Advance Praise

"Micka-Foos pulls no punches, shrouding these narratives in gloom … Gripping, sharply written tales that are rich in metaphor and atmosphere."

— *Kirkus Reviews*

"Literary in its language, astute in its psychological contrasts and considerations, and hard-hitting in its diverse examples of women under psychological siege, *It's No Fun Anymore* is thoroughly engrossing and completely empowering."

— D. Donovan, Senior Reviewer, *Midwest Book Review*

"Brittany Micka-Foos shows us the short story at its best: visceral, unflinching, and nail-biting. In these stories, the women protagonists bare the scars of childbirth and motherhood on their bodies and wear their anxieties on their sleeves, hyper attuned to the dangerous world around them and willing, if not always prepared, to do battle. If you want a collection that will bring a gun to a knife fight, this is the one. Unafraid and unapologetic, my only complaint was that I reached the end too soon."

— Gwen E. Kirby, author of *Shit Cassandra Saw*

"*It's No Fun Anymore* is a bracing read, a fearless collection that's willing to get weird and push the boundaries. These stories are incisive and visceral depictions of mothers on the brink. Each one digs into the real, beating heart of its characters, in all their messiness, anger, and humor. Brittany Micka-Foos is a gifted writer with an eye for the little details that make stories come alive."

— Tom McAllister, author of *How to Be Safe*

"I love the women in Brittany Micka-Foos's *It's No Fun Anymore*. One's husband complains to her, 'You see the sinister in everything.' What he views as a criticism is to me a testament to her savvy and her charm. These characters' all-too-familiar anxieties about the human world and about their abilities to cope with and thrive in that world lead them to test themselves in ways that put me on edge, made me laugh out loud, and caused me to recognize myself again and again."

— Michelle Ross, author of *They Kept Running* and *Shapeshifting*

"A beautiful, haunting collection that courageously tackles the societal constraints so many women and mothers experience, the complexity of relationships, and the lingering residue of childhood trauma and male violence. Full of exquisite details and profoundly human characters, this gripping collection peels back layers with masterful care and makes us see ourselves."

— Jennifer Case, author of *We Are Animals*

"In Brittany Micka-Foos's extremely impressive debut short story collection, younger women, wives and mothers—some married, some not—contend with their relationships with the men in their lives and, in some cases, their relationships with their own bodies. The collection delights with its subtleties, dark hints, and surprises. The author's voice is probing, questioning, and compassionate. Every story in *It's No Fun Anymore* drew me in and left me thinking and caring about the characters long after I finished the book."

— Lynn Levin, author of *House Parties* and *The Minor Virtues*

"Alternating between poignant, grim, and sometimes haunting stories, *It's No Fun Anymore* cuts to the core of all our deepest fears about being a woman in the 21st century. In stark prose, Micka-Foos makes you feel the immediacy of her characters' experience as they navigate motherhood, career, love, and getting out of bed each morning. Every story invites you to wrestle with the choices you'd make in the same situation, and that's where the real fun begins."

— Alexandria Faulkenbury, author of *Somewhere Past the End*

It's No Fun Anymore

It's No Fun Anymore

Stories

Brittany Micka-Foos

Apprentice
House Press
Loyola University Maryland

First Edition

Casebound ISBN: 978-1-62720-584-9
Paperback ISBN: 978-1-62720-585-6
Ebook ISBN: 978-1-62720-586-3

Cover & Internal Design by Molly Clement
Promotional Development by Olivia Cresser
Editorial Development by Natalie Misyak
Author Photo by Madison Bay Photography

Published by Apprentice House Press

Apprentice
House Press
Loyola University Maryland

Loyola University Maryland
4501 N. Charles Street, Baltimore, MD 21210
410.617.5265
www.ApprenticeHouse.com
info@ApprenticeHouse.com

For Karl

Contents

The Experiment

Leah and her husband, Derek, started The Experiment the day the Morristown police located the little girl's body in Slidell Creek. The girl had been missing for a week before she was found in the shallow creek bed, naked except for her socks. Her name was Gracie Lynn Abbot, and she was seven years old. Leah's own daughter, Skylar, had just turned six in June.

*

The Experiment was conceived in September, before Leah had ever heard of Gracie Lynn. It was just after Leah's thirty-sixth birthday, and she was slipping into another self-help spiral. Leah had too much time on her hands since Skylar started kindergarten. Every day after the school bus left, Leah would go to her writing desk until she began to resent it—the glaring white papers, the blankness of her laptop screen. To fill the space, she turned to a revolving door of self-help books and their gimmicky, all-too-revealing titles: *Ten Steps to Resurrect Your Marriage; Motherhood and the Search for Meaning; The Co-Dependency Workbook.*

When it became too much, her mind conjured up horrible scenarios for distraction, things that made her sick to her stomach. She'd picture Skylar's kindergarten teacher when she and Derek would have sex. Leah would imagine Mr. Conway, that vile man, his squarish body under her, that brick of a face looking up through a mesh of wet, thinning hair. She imagined him panting. She imagined his teeth: broad, brutal things. In some way, this satisfied her. As though she could stave off the dread of boredom with cheap horrors of her own creation.

But they never lasted long enough, these distractions. So, Monday through Friday, Leah returned to her books. She knew better, knew they made her irritable and dissatisfied, but she did it anyway. She read them by the dozen, piled high on her writing desk, spines discreetly turned towards the wall. She read aimlessly until she encountered *Magical Womanhood: The Subdued Power of the Feminine*. On the cover, a young woman wearing a red hood peered into the darkness, eyes wide and round like pennies. The book jacket touted "a return to traditional values. Women are more powerful, more capable when they remain at home." This, Leah thought, is *too much*. Then again, after Skylar's birth, it had been Leah who'd stayed home with the baby, Leah who'd quit her job while Derek retained his dentistry practice. Leah had welcomed the break: the long hours and stress of office life weren't the best fit for her temperament. Their arrangement was only meant to be temporary, until Leah found more fulfilling work. So, Leah stayed home for five years. Then, one day, Skylar went to kindergarten. Leah came back to a quiet, empty house and realized she was unemployed.

*

In September, when Leah sheepishly opened *Magical Womanhood* for the first time, little Gracie Lynn was out on a bike ride from which she'd never return. Of course, Leah didn't know this at the time—she heard it on the local news the next day, saw the "MISSING" posters on telephone poles, in the window of the Texaco on the way into town.

As concerned community members organized search parties to survey nearby wooded areas, and Gracie Lynn's parents pled for answers during daily press conferences, Leah hit the book's halfway point. She began reading the more ridiculous passages aloud to Derek in bed: "So-called 'Women's Lib' has promised much, but robbed us of everything. Only by rekindling those sacred feminine powers—a cheerful disposition, a childlike perspective, and an obedient soul—can a woman gain her natural heart's desire: the unconditional love of a man." *Isn't this bonkers?* Leah would say to Derek, and they'd laugh, but she continued reading. "There is covert strength in submission. To observers, a magical woman is meek and demure, but inside her is the power of all creation. Just as her body nourishes her offspring, through her charms she cultivates her environment. Her childlike demeanor invokes an inborn need in a man to cherish, to protect. The result is a satisfying and secure domestic life." Leah would read until late, then study the shadow of her husband in the dark, wondering what was going on behind his closed eyes, what he whispered to himself in his sleep.

So, the idea of The Experiment grew in her mind, until it became an escape plan, a life jacket, a gleaming hook she had been waiting to sink into the soft skin of her body.

*

Leah had just finished Chapter 6 ("How to keep your husband from straying: Avoiding unwomanly criticism") when she approached Derek with the idea of The Experiment. He was washing the dishes. Their dishwasher had been broken for weeks. Neither knew how to fix it; neither wanted to pay to get it repaired.

"It's a good idea," Leah said, as she carried a stack of dishes to the sink.

"Are you kidding? Because of that 'Mystic Woman' book?"

"Magical Womanhood."

"They tried that, Leah. It was called the 1950s," Derek said, plunging his hands into the soapy water.

"I need something to write about, and this feels timely."

"What happened to your novel? About the neurotic housewife?"

"It's not going anywhere."

"You've barely started!"

Leah frowned. "You can't reject this out of hand. It's not fair. Not when we haven't talked about it."

"What's there to talk about?" Derek sloshed around in the dirty water, searching for silverware.

"It's a *good* idea. I read this article about a journalist who spent an entire year living like women did in biblical times. She grew her hair long, made her own clothes. She even slept outside in a tent during her period."

"And what about that makes you think this is a good idea?"

"She wrote a whole book about it! A bestseller—about the tensions between feminism and religion. Her reckoning with misogyny."

"So, you want to write a bestseller about being a magical housewife?"

"I do think it would make a good book..." How could she explain the whole of it? The shameful need to feel in control of something. Anything.

Derek laughed. Leah was surprised as tears began welling up. She hated feeling misunderstood.

"Don't laugh at me," she said, in a way that came out more plaintive than she'd wanted. She took a breath to reset, steady her tone: "When you laugh like that, I feel like you aren't listening to me." She tried couching it the way that Terri, their couples thera-pist, had advised. *When you do this, I feel that...*

"I'm just being honest. I'm supposed to be honest, right? The idea sounds awful."

"Seriously, Derek, you're this dismissive? After everything?"

He put down the plate he was scrubbing. "Fuck, Leah, what do you want me to say?" Leah straightened her spine, bracing against his stare. Then his shoulders slackened, almost imperceptibly. "Okay," he said. "We can do it, if it means that much to you. If you think it's a good idea."

"I do. It'll be fun." She smiled, though she felt less convinced with each word.

Derek shrugged. "So, what do I have to do?"

Just like that, Leah started The Experiment. Hours later, police dogs found Gracie Lynn's body pinned facedown beneath a floating log.

*

Leah committed to the cause. She affixed a scarf around her head (she thought it made her look more maternal) and donned her best approximation of a house dress: a floral, billowy number. That first morning, the house was empty, quiet, and cluttered. She steeled herself for a long overdue housecleaning. This part wasn't strictly mandatory ("You can be a charming wife without being the perfect housekeeper, but it helps!"). Leah just wasn't sure where else to begin. She felt the whole day open wide before her, a vast, yawning mouth. She started sweeping crumbs off the floor.

It was almost noon by the time she finished the kitchen. She was avoiding the chickens, as usual. Last year, she had read about the benefits of backyard chickens on a parenting blog. There was something about those bright and tidy images: a blonde, barefoot mother and her brood, throwing feed to a cluster of chickens at their ankles, awash in the golden light of early morning. It screamed, GOOD MOTHERING. ALL-NATURAL. PEACE AND LOVE. It harkened back to a certain simplicity, a self-sufficiency that soothed. Leah had pestered Derek for months after. "It'll teach Skylar about the circle of life," she said. "It's so much healthier! Wouldn't you feel better knowing where your eggs come from?" Derek demurred; he didn't want the hassle or the mess.

And he didn't even eat eggs, thought it disgusting and cruel. Leah didn't really like eggs either, but goddamn it, she wanted those chickens so badly.

She wanted those chickens like she had wanted another child, once. Maybe still did, in some closed-off part of her mind. Being an only child seemed unfair for Skylar, and lonely. And there was something else, that vacancy in Leah's life that she sometimes wondered whether, just possibly, another child could fill. She'd hear other women say, upon the birth of their second or third child, "Our family felt complete after that." Some perfect number: was that all there was to it?

Reluctantly, Leah moved outside to survey the chicken coop. It needed cleaning, she noted with disgust. It always needed cleaning. Animals were so messy—they never show that in the photos—and chickens especially. All the shit and feed and dirty feathers, not to mention the rodents they attracted. Leah would step outside twice a day to feed them and, each time, she would think: *This has all been a terrible mistake.* Leah pushed the thought, the rising panic, back down. *No going back,* she told herself. *These are your babies now.*

It was Derek who had put his foot down about the second child. Not for his sake, he maintained: he loved children, took to fatherhood as naturally as anything. But for Leah's. It was Leah who'd had the difficult pregnancy; Leah who had suffered post-partum, her anxiety soaring to new levels after Skylar's birth. As if they'd dragged Skylar out of her, only to replace the fetus with this clawing fear, this black hole, fragile as a newborn's fontanelle. In the first years of Skylar's life, fear was the constant refrain: *What have I done? What have I done?* There was SIDS and croup and RSV. There were falls and sharp corners and choking hazards, thousands of unthinkable ways to injure and maim her tiny body.

Who would bring a child into this? It wasn't until Skylar turned four that the darkness seemed to lift a bit. Leah hadn't forgotten, but she secretly hoped that, a second time, things would be different. In fact, she wanted the opportunity to prove she could do it, this essential task of mothering—not just shuffle her way through it, overmedicated and dumb, but to revel in it. Or perhaps, more than that, she wanted Derek to want that for her, to reassure her she was capable and worthy. But the reassurance never came, and Leah knew better than to ask for it. Instead, she got chickens. A messy, boring consolation prize. Six hens and more eggs than she knew what to do with.

*

After the police found Gracie Lynn, Leah started walking Skylar to school. Safer than the bus, Leah reasoned, and it meant less idle time around the house. The leaves splintered under their feet as Leah and Skylar approached the elementary school grounds. Leah saw Mr. Conway leaning against the frame of the open classroom door with his arms crossed. His bright orange cable-knit sweater. His unnaturally white teeth. Bone white. Veneers, in Derek's professional opinion. *He's not fooling anyone. Nobody's teeth are that white.*

The classroom windows were decorated with paper jack-o-lanterns and black cats, silhouettes of wild-haired witches riding broomsticks. Tissue-paper ghosts swayed beneath the air duct.

"Good morning, Skylar," Mr. Conway bellowed, as Skylar slipped past him into the classroom. Leah thought she saw Skylar flinch. Mr. Conway smiled as though he hadn't noticed.

"Good morning," Leah said, forcing a smile of her own. "The room looks so festive."

"It's my favorite time of year," he said blandly. Behind him hung the jack-o-lanterns, dozens of black-hole mouths mimicking him.

He pulled out a square of paper from the back pocket of his jeans and handed it to Leah.

"The school's having a memorial for Gracie Lynn next Wednesday. We're encouraging parents to attend, if they can. Afterwards, there'll be a resource fair to connect with professionals who can provide further services."

"Services?" Leah imagined morticians, embalmers, grave diggers.

"Psychological services. Counseling."

"Oh, of course."

Leah took the small flyer from him. It had a pixelated graphic of a rose and nearly unreadable cursive font: "In Honor of the Precious Memory of Gracie Lynn Abbot."

"Leah—" Mr. Conway said suddenly, taking a step closer. "I wanted to ask how things are going at home. I know it's a difficult time."

Leah stared at him, a dangling, construction-paper "Boo" framing his head from behind.

"Skylar's such a bright girl," he said, finally. "But she keeps her cards close to the vest. I wonder if she would benefit from a little help processing recent events."

Leah craned her head to peer into the classroom. Skylar was sitting crossed-legged on the alphabet rug near the opposite wall. She picked at the carpet fibers, her eyes locked on Mr. Conway.

"Is there a problem?" Leah asked.

"Does Skylar ever talk with you about Gracie?"

"Not really. She didn't know her, so. I mean, we've talked about it. I think she's curious..."

"Which is normal."

Leah nodded solemnly. He was standing close enough that she could smell his breath, hot and earthy.

"Still," Mr. Conway continued, "she might find it helpful to talk to someone. A professional." He reached into his breast pocket this time and handed her a small business card: Mindscape Family and Child Psychology.

"Right," Leah said, focusing her eyes on the card. "Thanks."

"Of course," he said, his mouth open, teeth wet and gleaming.

*

"Can you believe that Mr. Conway thinks Skylar needs therapy?" Leah said to Derek after dinner. Derek sat reading *The Morristown Herald* while Leah cleared the dishes from the dining room table. He didn't look up. Leah continued, "God, he's such a weird man... isn't there something off about him?"

"Other than the veneers?"

"Why would a guy like that become a kindergarten teacher?"

"Guy like what?" Derek said, smirking from behind the paper.

"He's not particularly nice, right? Does he even like kids?"

"So now you have a problem with male kindergarten teachers," Derek said, matter-of-factly. "Or is this part of The Experiment?"

"I do *not* have a problem with male kindergarten teachers." Leah turned to face him. "It's him. He's too strict, for starters. Skylar doesn't like him."

"She said that?"

"No, but that's the impression I get. She kind of...shirks away from him. He can be a little gruff."

"Well, maybe it's good for her. A bit of tough love."

"The way he talks—it rubs me the wrong way. It's so condescending. I mean, come on, do you think Skylar needs a shrink?"

"Well," Derek said as he folded the newspaper. "It's not the worst idea."

"I think he just likes the power trip."

"What power trip?"

"Telling me I'm a shitty mom. You should have heard it: the way he kept saying, *professional*."

"I think you're taking this too personally."

What the fuck do you know about it? Leah thought. She swallowed, turning back to the sink and picking up the sponge. "Well, I guess that's that, then." *A magical woman can quietly accept criticism with grace and poise.*

"Leah—"

"No, it's fine. Point taken." She scrubbed a pan relentlessly with steel wool, trying to dissolve whatever had caked on the surface. *Grace and poise.*

Derek stared at her, his forehead creased.

"You're right," Leah said eventually. "I was taking it too personally. It's not about me."

Derek nodded slowly. "So, what about therapy?"

Leah smiled. "You decide."

"Very funny, Leah."

"I'm not joking."

"Doesn't the book say you're in charge of childrearing stuff?"

"Big decisions are you, remember?"

"That's ridiculous. We should decide together."

Leah put down the pan she was working on. "Derek, you promised me." She made sure to keep her smile fixed and her tone light.

"Yes, but, come on," Derek said, "I didn't anticipate child murder. I didn't anticipate our daughter being traumatized."

"Oh, I don't know that she's *traumatized*…"

"She talks about Gracie every damn day, Leah. This morning she asked if she was going to die when she's seven."

"She's curious. That's normal, right? She's normal. Sometimes she just says things. She told me when *I* die, I'm going to New

Jersey, so..."

"How can you be so glib about this?"

"I'm not! If you want my opinion, I think it's a little over-blown. I think Mr. Conway is trying to fit Skylar into a box of grieving she's not in."

"Or, he sees a side of her you don't."

I'm with her every goddamn day, asshole. Leah took a breath and composed herself.

"Maybe you're right. I don't necessarily trust his judgement, you know? But that's just my opinion—since you asked." She fixed her gaze out the dining room window, just above Derek's head. It was getting dark so early now.

"It seems like he's doing his job. Looking out for Skylar." Derek continued softly, "It couldn't hurt to make one appointment."

Leah smiled.

"Alright, Leah? I'm deciding. Let's make the appointment."

Leah said nothing, bit the inside of her cheek, still smiling.

*

The following morning, the Mindscape Psychology business card sat atop Leah's pile of writing notes. Instead of making the call, she went outside to clean the coop, the lesser of two evils.

Five of the six chickens moved around the yard, dutifully peck-ing the ground for bugs. The most aggressive of the hens, the puni-tive ringleader Petunia, was absent.

Petunia was a bully and a cannibal, and Leah hated her. After about a month in the coop, Petunia had started eating the eggs. Leah would come outside in the mornings and find a carpet of broken shells surrounded by five grieving hens. Separate from the rest was Petunia, strutting around: preening, unconcerned, and satiated.

When Leah researched the matter online, she learned

egg-eating was evidence of a vitamin deficiency. Or a symptom of overcrowding or boredom or pure curiosity. *Once they find out how good they taste, it's hard to stop them,* Leah had read. The suggested remedy was draconian: clip the offending chicken's beak with shears, removing just the knife-like tip to make it more difficult to break the eggs. *Just like trimming your fingernails,* said one website. Others maintained it was a *mutilation, psychologically scarring, unnecessarily cruel.* But Leah was desperate: the five other chickens were becoming disconsolate.

One summer day, Leah had knelt down in the dry grass, clutching Petunia in one hand, kitchen scissors in the other. Normally, Petunia twitched and struggled whenever Leah would handle her, pecking at her hands or whatever she could reach. But, that day, Petunia had been soft and limp in her grip, easily pliable. Leah opened the scissors and placed the tip of Petunia's beak between the shaking blades. *One quick, clean cut,* Leah coached herself. *Just don't hit the vein. Please don't hit the vein.* Leah pictured the bloody, open stump of a beak, imagined an assembly line of grotesque chickens with asymmetrical mandibles. She put down the scissors and watched Petunia strut away.

Instead, Leah took the coward's way out, replacing some eggs with golf balls, which Petunia would inevitably peck, bruising her beak. Enough of a lesson to last until the cycle repeated itself: a cruel practical joke to restore the peace temporarily.

This morning, when Leah looked into the coop, six shiny Titleists lay undisturbed in the nest box, where she had left them a week before. In the far corner was Petunia, huddled in a rigid, unnatural position. Her head lolled, and her comb looked brittle and white. *Shit.* Leah backed away from the coop. It smelled worse than usual. *Shit, shit, shit. Poor Petunia.* And then, once again, *what have I done?*

All day, Leah tried to forget about Petunia, even as her mind reeled through her past failings as a caretaker, the vital signs she had missed. By 4:50, Leah broke down and called Mindscape Family and Child Psychology. The receptionist was apologetic: "With the holidays coming up, we won't have anything open until mid-January at the earliest. It's the busy time of year, unfortunately."

"Would you like to be added to the waiting list?" the receptionist asked.

"I'll call back later," Leah replied, and hung up, awash in guilt and relief.

*

Leah said nothing to Derek that evening. Nothing of consequence, anyway. She didn't mention the phone call, or the sick chicken, or the increasingly bleak thoughts she was having. Chapter 2: "A magical woman is selfless. She will not burden her husband with womanly concerns. Remember, he is not interested in the minutiae of your day. He has enough on his plate: why not ask about his work instead?" Surprisingly, Leah agreed with this one, in principal. *Clean up your own mess,* she chided herself.

After putting Skylar to bed, Leah led Derek to the couch. She arranged the pillows behind his back and knelt down on the floor next to him. Methodically, she began to remove his socks, folding them next to her on the ground.

"Seriously, Leah, what is this?"

"I'm giving you a foot rub. Chapter 8: 'Be a kind and faithful servant to your husband.'"

"Aren't you sick of this right-wing garbage? This isn't you." Derek crossed, then uncrossed, his legs, shifting his body weight as though the cushions were made of glass.

"It's not right-wing—not specifically. Think of it as an opportunity to examine gender roles."

"It's ridiculous. You're making me uncomfortable."

"Derek, it's an experiment, remember? Just relax."

Leah was curled up on the floor at the foot of the couch, with her legs neatly tucked under her body, her peasant skirt splayed out around her. She tried to keep her voice breezy, like this was all a game. "Give me your feet, silly."

"This is too weird. Come on, come up on the couch. Sit next to me."

"Derek. Relax, okay? Close your eyes or something." She smiled at her husband. "What's that saying: lie back and think of England?"

She reached toward him. His leg was tensed as if primed to kick. At a loss, she started petting his foot—tentatively at first, before giving way to empty reflex. She was thinking about Skylar, and the appointment she couldn't bring herself to make. She was also thinking of Petunia. How long could a chicken live like that? Deep down, a part of her hoped Petunia would die overnight so she could quietly discard the body, clean up the mess, pretend Petunia never happened.

"How was your day?" Derek asked sleepily from the couch.

Leah smiled, cooed, "It was nothing special. How was work?"

*

Petunia did not die overnight. In a final show of defiance, Petunia survived, if barely. She had lost most of her feathers, revealing slimy, red sores on her balding body. A thick yellow liquid oozed onto the floor of the coop. What if Petunia's affliction, whatever it was, spread to the other chickens? To the eggs? To Skylar? *What have you done, Leah? What terrible thing have you unleashed on your family?*

When Derek came home from the clinic, Leah broke down in tears before he had even set his keys on the entryway table. "What's wrong?" he asked, eyes widening. "Where's Skylar?"

"I'm so sorry," Leah sputtered. "I've done something terrible."

Derek moved to the kitchen and glanced at Skylar, who was sitting at the table eating from a large bowl of strawberries and listening, intently, but without apparent concern. "Leah, what are you talking about?"

"Petunia's sick. Really sick. I think she's dying."

Derek exhaled. "Okay Leah, calm down. I'm sure it's fine."

"Derek, I'm telling you, she's *dying*," Leah said between sobs. "She's dying and—"

"Not so loud, Leah, okay?" Derek said under his breath.

"Dying? Mom, who's dying?" asked Skylar.

"One of the chickens isn't feeling well, sweetie," Derek said, putting his shoes back on. "But it's okay. I'll go take a look."

When Derek came back inside, he said quietly, "We need to take her to the vet, Leah."

"It's too late for the vet!" Leah cried. "What can a vet do at this point? Charge us a bunch of money for a mercy killing?"

"What's a mercy killing?" asked Skylar, her mouth full.

Derek hovered at the back door, hand suspended over the knob. "Maybe the vet could—"

"No—no vet!" Leah covered her face with her hands. "Please. I don't want anyone to see how bad it is."

Derek sighed. "Okay. Maybe we see what happens overnight?"

"Derek," Leah said. "She's suffering." Leah wiped her nose with her hand. "I think we have to—take care of it."

"We?" said Derek.

"Do what? Take care of what?" said Skylar. Red juice dripped down her chin.

Leah took a breath. "I'll do it. I just need to think." Leah moved to the kitchen and started opening drawers, pulling out various lengths of knives from their sheaths.

"Leah, what are you doing?"

"Looking for the sharp knife."

Skylar leaned over the table. "Mom, what are you going to do?"

"Leah, come on. Stop."

Leah put the blade of a chef's knife against her forearm, gently pressed it into her skin. "Why are all our blades so dull?" she wondered aloud.

"Leah, stop!" Derek shouted. Skylar's head whipped back towards him. "Let me handle it, okay? Stop."

"She's my chicken, and it's my fault..."

"Leah, I said I'll handle it. It's my job, remember?"

Leah looked at her husband. He was still wearing his dentist's coat, stiff and pristinely white even after a full day at the clinic. His surgical mask hung limp around his neck. Slowly, she put down the knife. "How are you going to do it?" she asked.

Derek shook his head. "I'll figure something out," he said. "Keep Skylar inside."

Fifteen minutes later, he emerged from the garage. He had stripped down to his undershirt and boxers. His hands were red. Leah scanned his face for some sign of what had happened, but only found a few splatters of blood on his cheek and a disquieting blankness.

He gave a curt little nod as he passed, making his way upstairs. It was done.

"Mom, what did Dad do?" Skylar asked, jumping up from the table.

"Nothing, honey," Leah said. "Finish your dinner."

*

That night, in bed, Leah rested her head on Derek's chest. He hadn't said a word to her since he'd come back inside. The silence

16

lay heavy between them like an accusation.

"This whole thing's ridiculous, isn't it?" Leah offered. Derek said nothing, so Leah continued. "I feel awful about...making you do that."

"You didn't make me do anything," he said.

"Still. My chickens, my massacre. It's only fair."

Derek took a deep breath. "I was happy to do it. I mean, not happy to do it, but it's nice to be able to do something...to show you can trust me. That I'm not *that guy* anymore."

"Not that guy..." Leah repeated.

He turned to face her, and continued, "I hope this means something to you."

In the darkness of the room, he looked like an intruder. Like he could be anyone. "I want you to know what I'm capable of," he said.

"This whole thing...it's not about you being capable. You know that, right?"

Derek sighed and leaned back on the pillow, facing the ceiling. "Poor thing." He swallowed. "She wasn't dead. After everything. It was just like they always say: she kept running around in circles with her head hanging by this thin piece of skin. Just rattling around. I didn't expect so much blood. She kept running..."

Leah drew her hand to her throat. "I didn't think it would be like that," she said weakly.

"What did you think it would be like?" he said, an edge in his voice.

Leah didn't answer. She didn't know.

"It was the humane thing to do," Derek said at last, without much conviction.

"Where's the body?"

Derek paused to let out a breath. "I threw it in the garbage."

"Of course," she said, like a conspirator. "Thanks for handling it."

"Just—" Derek paused. "No one should go in the garage right now. I didn't get a chance to clean up."

"Oh, I can—"

"Don't." He rolled over and away from her.

Leah couldn't sleep. She kept thinking about Petunia. It was over, and she should feel relieved, but instead there was only that steady thrum: *Wrong, wrong, wrong.* She could feel the pulse of it inside of her, like a heartbeat under the floorboards.

Beside her, Derek appeared to be asleep. Occasionally, he would snore or mutter something indecipherable. He was noisier than usual tonight. Leah laid there listening to him, trying to divine some meaning in his murmurings. His breathing grew heavier, ragged—a choking, tangled sound. Leah couldn't see his face in the dark. She put her hand on his back, rubbing it in small, halting circles. He turned on his side to face her, took her hand and held it for a beat. In the next, he was on top of her, legs straddling her waist, bearing down with the full weight of his body. Leah coughed in surprise. She wiggled underneath him, but her arms were pinned under his thighs.

"Come on, Derek, let me out," she said, laughing. He didn't budge. "I can't do much like this," Leah added. Derek grunted but said nothing, just slid his body up further until the head of his penis reached her lips, against her closed teeth. She turned her head to the side. "Very funny," she said. Derek knew she didn't like blow jobs, that they aggravated her jaw, which was compromised from grinding her teeth over the years. He would sometimes pester her about it when he was drunk, which wasn't often. Had he been drinking tonight? Leah didn't think so. "Seriously, Derek, this is uncomfortable," she said, struggling to get up on her elbows. He held her down.

"This is supposed to be fun," he said, his voice high-pitched, mimicking her. "Just relax, okay? Lie back and think of England."

*

The next morning, Derek was stony as he ate breakfast and prepared for work. At the front door, Leah handed him the bagged lunch that she had prepared and his car keys. As he grabbed them, he reminded her, "Don't go in the garage, alright?" She rubbed the side of her face. "Alright, Leah?" he repeated.

Leah nodded.

Then he thrust his hand into her hair and pulled her in for a deep kiss, cradling her head like a precious object. He left without saying goodbye.

Leah nursed her jaw as she watched Derek's car disappear down the street. The need to see Petunia nagged at her, a snake in her ear. As Skylar ate breakfast, Leah slipped out to the garage. It smelled of sawdust and iron. First, she saw the shovel by the door, bits of crimson fluff stuck to the blade. There was blood everywhere: streaking the walls, fanning up towards the ceiling, congealed in dark puddles on the concrete floor. Red footprints led to the tool chest, to the garbage can. An assortment of other instruments: a hatchet; some pruning shears; her sad, bent gardening trowel. All used, some still slick and wet. There were concentric circles of red at her feet, loop after loop, a Satanic, dizzying path. Leah opened the garbage can. She removed a thin, bent sheet of carboard off the top, revealing Petunia's headless body among the discarded juice boxes and apple cores. Leah's eyes watered from the stench, but she couldn't turn away. Petunia looked shrunken, crumpled in on herself, her once-bright coat now gummy with gore. *My poor baby.* Leah reached out to lift Petunia and cradle her carcass. So stiff, so light. Leah stood there rocking Petunia in the garage, inhaling the stale air and scent of blood. From the dining room, Skylar was calling for her. Leah returned Petunia to the trash can, closed the lid softly, and slunk back into the house.

*

Leah walked Skylar down the tree-lined streets that led to the elementary school. She ignored the weather-beaten "MISSING CHILD" posters stapled on every other telephone pole. Gracie Lynn's smiling face flapping in the wind, her shining hair, her bright smile. On the pole closest to the crosswalk, there was a new poster next to Gracie Lynn: "2 out of every 5 female murder victims are killed by an intimate partner. STOP THE SILENCE. REPORT DOMESTIC VIOLENCE."

"Mom, who's going to take care of me?" Skylar asked as the school came into view.

"What do you mean, sweetie? I take care of you. Dad and I both do."

"But who will take care of me when you die?"

"Well, by then you'll be a grown up." Leah tried to smile. "That means you can take care of yourself."

Skylar looked down at her shoes as she walked. "What if a person doesn't want to be buried?" she asked.

"What if a person doesn't want to be buried?"

"Yeah. A dead person. I don't want to be put in the ground when I'm dead."

"Oh, well, there are other options, I guess." *We could stuff you in a garbage can.*

"What options?"

Leah looked away. "Let's talk about it when you're older, okay?"

"Mom, I need to know now," Skylar said, tugging on Leah's arm.

"Well, it's your body, so you can pretty much do whatever you want with it."

Skylar smiled. "I want to stay in our house when I'm dead. In my room."

"Okay, maybe you can do that."

"Okay," Skylar said. She stopped to scrape the bottom of her shoe against some blackened bubblegum on the pavement, exposing a flash of pink beneath before moving on.

*

Leah grasped Skylar's hand in hers as they entered the gymnasium. In her other hand, she held a small basket of eggs. No one had told her what to bring, but she sensed she should bring something and hadn't felt up to baking. Several uneven rows of folding chairs were arranged in front of the gym's pull-out stage. At the foot of the stage was a black music stand and a lone microphone. Next to that was a large picture of Gracie Lynn that appeared to have been printed last-minute at Kinko's. It sat awkwardly atop a folding chair.

As Mr. Conway approached, Skylar ran off to one side of the gym, slipping into a group of girls huddled around a robotic, singing doll. Leah wanted to call her back, but didn't.

"So glad you could make it, Leah," said Mr. Conway, smiling at something in the distance. He was wearing an off-white turtleneck, and Leah could see the sweat stains creeping up through the thin material under his arms. "I hope our little memorial service for Gracie Lynn will bring a sense of closure for the kids. So important in times like these."

"I brought eggs," Leah said, offering them up to him. She ran her eyes over the basket one last time, checking for golf balls.

"That's very kind," he said, without taking the basket. "Skylar speaks fondly of her pet chickens."

What else has she told you? Leah searched for some deeper meaning in his lingering smile. She kept the basket extended awkwardly between them. Around them, more parents—mothers, grandmothers, perhaps a few nannies—filed in with their children and baked goods.

"Well, I'll go put these with the rest of the food," Mr. Conway said, sliding his tongue across his teeth.

The fluorescent lights flickered, and everyone moved towards the stage. Leah took a seat in the front row. Most of the students sat cross-legged on the sticky, bare floor. Some adults lingered on the edges of the room, near doorways. Every so often, someone would enter from the back of the gym, letting the harsh midmorning light in through the double doors.

Leah started counting. Mr. Conway. The principal. Another man in a suit. Three men amid a room of women and children.

One of the first-grade teachers, Ms. Spofford, spoke solemnly about the importance of community, how small acts of kindness mean the world. *Some community,* Leah thought. *A child was murdered here.* The man in the suit introduced himself as the school psychologist, whose door was always open for any kid—or parent—who needed to talk. As the choir performed "I Believe I Can Fly," battery-operated candles were passed out to kids in the front row, then promptly confiscated once the second row turned riotous. Leah watched Skylar, who sometimes swayed to the music, other times hunched over to pick at her shoes. During the final chorus, the picture of Gracie Lynn fell from its perch. Leah flinched as it smacked the floor, its echo reverberating against the walls.

Cardboard Gracie remained facedown throughout the choir's off-key rendition of "Stand By Me." Leah imagined Mr. Conway carrying the cardboard poster to the dumpster after the assembly. Garbage, and more garbage. Leah scanned the faces of the women around her. They appeared entranced. *No, I won't be afraid...no, I won't be afraid.* Some women sung along in a quiet, focused monotone, chant-like. Leah was struck by how confined the auditorium was: the suffocating, desperate quality of the air and the bodies surrounding her. The too-few exits. And then, there was Skylar, in the middle of the room, smiling and small. Six years old with gum stuck to the sole of her shoe. Something about that was almost unbearable to consider. *Why can't I keep you safe?* Leah thought, over and over in an incessant loop, until she realized she was shrieking.

*

That night, Leah was folding laundry. A dent in a daunting backlog of housework. She balanced halfhearted piles on top of her desk, burying barely-started drafts and errant notes. She was still feeling shaky, unsure of herself. When she put her hand to her neck, it felt tense and swollen. Maybe she was coming down with something.

"I heard you made a bit of a scene today. At the memorial," Derek said from the bathroom.

Leah looked up from a stack of shirts towards the open bathroom door. Her husband was shaving. His eyes gleamed in the mirror as they met hers.

"Skylar's teacher called me," he continued.

"Mr. Conway called you?"

"He was worried about you, Leah. And worried about Skylar."

Leah forced a smile.

"Are you going to tell me what happened, or do I have to pry it out of you?" He grimaced as he tilted his head to get at the underside of his chin. "If you have a full-on breakdown in public, you have to expect people to ask questions." His voice was distant and gravelly, like a hardboiled detective in an old movie.

"I didn't have a *breakdown*," Leah said.

"Mr. Conway said you were howling. Like hysterics."

Leah shook her head. "It wasn't like that."

"I'm worried about you," Derek continued. "You seem anxious, ever since Skylar started school. Have you been feeling anxious again?"

Leah watched her husband in the mirror, how deftly he whipped the razor over the thin skin of his neck, the scrape of the blade. Chop, chop.

"I think we should have a funeral for Petunia," she said at last.

Derek laughed. "Don't you think that's a little much? You know Skylar's going to ask how she died. What are you going to say? Dad slaughtered her in the garage?"

Leah bit her lip. "If we don't say anything, then Petunia's just this big, blank question mark. That feels so wrong. Like, she's disposable because she's a chicken?"

"She *is* disposable, Leah. If she'd been healthy when she died, you'd have served her to Skylar for dinner."

"I—" Leah shook her head. "She deserved more than to be mutilated and thrown away."

"FUCK." Derek jerked his head back. "Can you get me a tissue, *please*?" he snapped, holding his fingers against his neck. Blood dripped onto the floor in long rivulets. Leah handed a wad over to him, watching helplessly as he sopped up the blood.

"I'm not the bad guy here," he continued, wiping his neck. "I'm not the one who wanted this. Any of it. Petunia, the experiment—it was your idea. You were dead set on it. Remember? How it was going to be a best-seller?"

"I didn't—"

"Do you think this is fun for me? You asked for it. Begged me. You wanted a man, and that's what you got."

"You think killing a chicken and throat-fucking your wife make you a man?"

"You're not the victim here!" He spat into the sink. "Look

around. You have it all. Anything you ask, you get. Chickens? Of course. A kid? You got it. Some half-baked idea, some silly experiment to make you feel like you're not wasting your life? Sure, sweetheart, why not!"

Leah took a step back. "Who *are* you?"

Derek let out a loud, gasping laugh. "Don't do that. You know me, Leah. I'm the guy who'd do anything for you. Anything— even this stupid experiment. Hell, I uprooted my practice, moved across the country to keep our family together. Doesn't that mean anything?"

"We moved out here to get away from the mess *you* made. We moved because I couldn't even go to the grocery store without hearing about her!"

"What am I supposed to do? What can I possibly do that I haven't done already?"

"How about you look in the mirror before asking me why I'm so goddamn anxious all the time?"

"You're anxious because you fuck up everything you touch. Everything. You can't handle your own life. You weren't happy at work, you're not happy staying home. So, you come up with these stupid ideas, and it's no surprise they don't work out. It always becomes too much, you fuck it up, and yet somehow, *I'm* the bad guy. Just like with Petunia, or with this idiotic experiment—"

"I just wanted—"

"No. This ends now. I'm done being the fall guy for your fuck-ups." Derek exhaled loudly and set the razor by the sink. "I need you to look me in the eye and tell me this whole experiment didn't go how you wanted."

"Fine," Leah said, leaning back against the door frame. "It's not what I wanted."

"I don't believe you."

Leah looked toward her husband. Over his shoulder, in the mirror, she saw her own slumped refection. "This isn't what I wanted!" she said louder.

"Well then, what was it?"

Leah shook her head. "I don't know. It was a mistake! I don't know what you want me to say."

"No, we've made it this far." He spoke each word slowly, deliberately. "I need to hear you say it. This whole thing was...?"

Leah blinked back the tears that threatened to obscure her vision. She tried again. "It was...my fault."

She watched his face soften. "Good girl," Derek said, wiping the last of the blood off his hands. "Now we can go back to normal."

"Normal?" Leah shook her head. "None of this is normal." She suddenly felt dizzy and slid to the ground, her back against the bathroom wall.

"Nothing is ever as bad as you think," Derek said gently.

"A little girl is dead. That could have been Skylar. And I can't protect her from—" Leah covered her mouth with her hands. *We embody these qualities because, without cultivating a man's affection, our world is one of fear and brutality. This is magical womanhood.*

Derek cocked his head and looked at Leah with an amused expression. Then, slowly, he moved closer, reached down, and touched her shoulder. She could smell his shaving cream wafting over her. It was overpowering, sickeningly sweet.

"Oh baby," he said, brushing the hair out of her face. "I thought you knew. They caught him. They caught Gracie's murderer. Some drifter, they arrested him this afternoon. It's over now."

He stood over her, cooing, "There's nothing to be afraid of. You're safe, you're safe, you're safe."

It's No Fun Anymore

"We shouldn't have come," I say to John as we edge past a procession of buoyant teens in *seifuku.* They hold each other by wrists and waists, all pleated skirts and knee-highs. Oversized red bows cling to their delicate throats.

A middle-aged man blocks their path, lanyard swinging around his neck, bald spot shining under the hotel chandelier. He extends his camera toward the girls, and they stack into a graceful pyramid, giggling. Some tilt their heads and stick out their tongues, others form hearts with their hands. The flash of the camera, and then they disappear, dispersed back into the crowd of the hotel lobby.

"Why wouldn't we come?" my husband replies, his smile tight and unyielding. "You love this." When I say nothing, he repeats, "*Mel,* you love this."

"This was a mistake," I say, tugging at my petticoat with one hand and holding our one-year-old, Bea, with the other. "I feel ridiculous."

"No," he says, without looking at me. "You look great."

"I look *old.*" My voice has an unrecognizable pitchiness to it. My jaw tightens, a vise.

*

I'm at least a decade older than the average convention-goer. Hell, most of these kids are in high school. They walk around in obscure, colorful costumes and speak loudly in slang. They carry their tiny devices, in tight groups or pairs, heads down and painfully oblivious to whatever's ahead. Every time I'm at one of these things, I start wishing I could go back to high school and do things differently. But here I am, a thirty-something *mother for chrissake* in a bubblegum wig and ill-fitting *otome kei* dress—the only one that fit after Bea's birth.

Who exactly are you supposed to be? I think as I catch my reflection in the lobby elevator. John, in street clothes as usual, presses on toward the rotunda.

"What do you want to do first?" he asks, still smiling. I shrug and relocate Bea to my other hip.

"Any interesting panels?" he continues, fishing around the plastic promotional bag for a program.

"No," I say. "Too stressful with Bea." A couple dressed in black-and-gold gilded kimonos passes us by, so close I can hear the layers of fabric rubbing against each other.

"You could go without us." John offers me the trifold paper. "We can entertain ourselves for an hour."

I shake my head and clutch harder to Bea.

"Okay, how about we check out the vendors' hall?"

"Let's just people-watch," I say.

John heads toward a pair of escalators in the center of the foyer. A large banner hangs above our heads: *Welcome to Tanoshii Con—Fun for all ages!* As we descend, I see the crowd slither below us, pulsing with adolescent energy. The unrelenting rattle of indistinct conversations. We move through the crowd to an adjacent hall, with its geometric arrangement of soft benches and side tables. I set Bea down next to me on a beige couch. She stares over me, eyes locked on a pair of furries reclining on a couch behind us. The orange fox tilts its head and waves tentatively. The red raccoon covers her eyes with oversized paws. *Peek-a-boo.* Bea howls with delight or fear, a new emotion I can't place. I move her onto my lap, waving a strand of my wig to capture her attention. I frown.

Animal suits or not, they're still strangers.

*

My scalp itches under the wig. I remember this hall from a few years ago, the first convention I brought John to. I went as Red Sonja, the she-devil with a sword. I wore an intricate metal bikini, which I made by weaving hundreds of aluminum scales together. A heaviness and a lightness at once. I couldn't walk three feet without getting stopped for a picture. I knew from past cons to avoid photo shoots: most of the so-called professionals with cameras just want to see you slap your ass or fondle yourself. But I was thrilled when a female photographer approached me. We cleared a space on one of the couches, which she covered with a black velvet blanket. Her assistant maintained a perimeter around the shoot. Behind the glare of the flash, I could see onlookers taking second-hand shots, and John, holding my bag, eyes on me. The photographer gently walked me through the standard poses. She instructed me to sit up tall and arch my back, to prop my arms behind me so that my stomach wouldn't bulge unflatteringly. "Happens to everyone," she said as I struggled to support my body weight with my forearms. "It feels unnatural, but looks great in photos."

She was right. The photos were transformative, polished and glossy. My face was unreadable and mine alone. I showed them to my sister Lacey when I came home for Christmas that year. I'm not sure why I did, or what I wanted her to see. She rolled her eyes.

We used to be close. But she had just gotten married, and had gone through her own sort of metamorphosis into a more ascetic, abstaining version of herself. I blamed it on her husband, whom she always referred to as "my husband," even though his name was Walter. As in, "my husband and I don't drink anymore," or "my husband and I are giving up masturbation for Lent." In our conversations, you'd think I was the younger sister. Later that same visit, as I left for the bar downtown, she asked what John (whom I'd been dating all of six months) would think.

"He trusts me. We trust each other."

She waved her hands as if shooing a fly. "A bar, Melanie? Do you think that's a good idea? When I married my husband, I made a vow that I wouldn't—" she paused, considering, "put my virtue in a compromising position."

"Virtue, seriously? I just want a drink."

She narrowed her eyes. "I don't go to bars alone. I don't visit men alone. I wouldn't want my husband to be tempted, and I extend the same courtesy to him." She folded her arms neatly across her chest.

I laughed. "Can you hear how ridiculous you sound? Besides, if John wanted to be with someone else, I'd rather know about it."

Lacey looked at me blankly, so I continued: "I wouldn't want him to avoid other women out of some duty to me. If he wanted to sleep with someone else, I'd want the kind of relationship where we could at least discuss it." I said this flippantly, as if off the top of my head, but the truth is I thought about it a lot. How could anyone guarantee they wouldn't fall in love with someone else? But honestly, I always figured it would be me.

"You mean an open relationship." Lacey crinkled her nose.

"No. But at least we'd have a *conversation* about it."

Lacey sighed. "Listen to me," she said, her voice softer. "I wouldn't open that can of worms. You'll regret it."

I shook my head and laughed too hard, as if that was the most ridiculous thing I'd ever heard. Then I left her there.

*

Lacey and I have always been different—I don't want to say that she has a chameleon-like personality, that she molds herself to whatever man she's currently attached to—but she does have a tendency to get caught up in things, to grasp just a little too tight. I can't blame her. I created my own orbit—the conventions and the costumes, my whole separate life in DC to define me—while she's stuck back home in Medford with the leftovers. And let me be clear: I left her there.

What I'm saying is, we both try, in our own imperfect way, to escape those long shadows that haunt us.

Now she's all-in on religion: parochial schools and drawn-out Sunday sermons. Her house is overflowing with babies. That's why she won't visit me in DC. "It's too far," she says. "I can't board a plane with three under five!" Plus, they've started growing their own food. I can't imagine it; I'm overwhelmed with just Bea and a trip to the grocery store. When John had to go to Atlanta on business, I thought I'd lose my mind. I didn't leave the house the entire four days. I just sat on the floor—padded with colorful, thin foam for Bea—surrounded by all those rattling, reflective baby toys, watching the hours melt away until darkness. Sometimes I wake up in the middle of the night and cry for no good reason. Those are the times I want to call Lacey and tell her, "I don't know who I am anymore," just to hear her tell me she remembers. I never call though. She has enough on her hands: her sprawling family, dark thoughts of her own. We aren't kids anymore.

My phone vibrates in my bag. Bea pulls at my wig, putting gobs of it into her mouth, imparting a sticky, white residue on the pink strands. More attendees walk by. I slump down under the weight of their fleeting attention. No one's interested in the three of us, I remind myself, not really.

More people gather at the hotel bar down the hall, attendees of drinking age. My breast milk leaks into the delicate fabric of the corset. Dry clean only. A damp reminder that it's time for Bea's next nursing session. I scan the room for a sign: someone like me, anyone else with a small child pulling at them. Of course, I see small children everywhere, sitting cross-legged on the faded carpets, with their inside jokes and plastic bags brimming with merchandise. A girl in a clingy, sequined dress and bright heels stumbles on a rug covering an electrical cord, rights herself with outstretched arms. She seems unbothered. Still, I can't shake this sense that everything is unsafe.

*

Last time I was here, the Red Sonja time, I drank at that very bar. Men would come up to me even though I was obviously with John. Even Batman removed his mask and sidled up next to the open seat on my left. He said I was beautiful and asked if he could buy me a drink. I told him I was with someone, offering up John on my right. Batman extended a congratulatory "well done, man," and bought me the drink anyway. As I sipped the gin and tonic, Batman turned his seat to face me, gray tights straddling both sides of my stool.

"Your costume is *fantastic*," he said, drawing out the word and then a breath. "You look real good: a solid eight."

John snorted his soda behind me. "An eight? Are you blind?"

Batman drew his hand to his chin and looked me up and down. "Okay. Eight point five."

John smiled, resting an elbow on the bar. "I'm guessing numbers aren't your strong suit."

Batman put his hands in the air, a gesture of mock surrender. "Eight point five's a compliment."

John shook his head and turned to face him. I leaned back, let them talk about me. I wasn't offended then. They fought back and forth across my shoulders, tiny insistent voices. I never said a word. I didn't need to. I stood for myself. I was a thing beyond words, an untouchable monument. That's what I thought, at least. Three years ago to the day.

The best thing about those weekends was the sex. I kept my wig on even though it itched like hell, smelled of stale sweat the next day. When John pulled up my skirt from behind and held me down against the hotel bed, I felt like someone else. I still think about the way his thumbs felt pressing deep into the small of my back. There were mirrors on all four walls, a mirror on the ceiling—hundreds of versions of ourselves refracted into oblivion. Of course I knew it was escapist, of course it was a fantasy world. That's why I cried Sunday afternoon at the end of the con, when the vendors were closing up shop, and kids sat on the curb with their suitcases and oversized stuffed animals waiting for their parents to shuttle them back to suburbia. I wore my costume back home and into the evening, even though the apartment doorman stared at me dumbly, jaw gaping, telling me Halloween was over months ago.

*

A woman walks by us in a veil and iridescent bikini, her cleavage an outpouring of glitter. Her hips sway as she walks past, and a hundred tiny bells chime. She looks light enough to walk on air. I will myself not to look at John, lest my mind try to divine some sort of meaning from his gaze, wherever it might fall. I stare down at her bare feet—perfect, painted little things—and I feel something in my stomach uncoil, raw and hungry. Once, this had been so easy. At the burlesque show at the con in Baltimore, John and I sat in the second row. We watched the opening act, a woman covered in neon body paint, spinning around in the dark, confetti falling from the ceiling. Our unblinking eyes on her body, alive and swaying like a snake. Hypnotic, honest fun. It had been fun, hadn't it?

A small boy dressed as Captain America crosses the room, flanked by his parents. Neither adult is dressed up. They pass by us wide-eyed and hesitant. Their movements through the crowd have a shirking, ovine quality. I don't make eye contact. Instead, I think:

would I bring Bea here when she's older? I'm briefly thankful for her limited awareness, for how small the surface of her world is.

I remember the soccer mom with the severe bob from my last time here, and how quickly she'd covered her son's eyes when I stepped into the elevator as Red Sonja. The feeling of her gaze boring into me, that silent accusation, the hot molten core of her stare. I fixed my gaze straight ahead at the elevator doors, smiling at myself all the way down. What else could I do? Another time, another con: a man walked up to me and said, "nice tits," cordially as one might say "nice weather." He looked me dead in the eye, stood too close. He was smiling so I could see his teeth. His daughter, eight or nine, held his hand, dark eyes on me. He kept smiling as I said nothing. I wasn't even wearing a costume.

Maybe the weight of all the things I never say is catching up with me. I used to think just keeping my head high was the statement, the strength. Maybe not. Maybe I've taken the easy way out.

*

The Captain America family disappears into the crowd, swallowed up.

"Can we please leave?" I say to John.

"It's only four. We just got here."

I watch the hordes swell over his shoulder. I see them hover, then surround a girl wearing a white cape. She disappears in the flashes of cameras, requests spoken and unspoken.

I repeat, my pitch rising: "John, can we please leave?"

John sighs and turns away, gathering up Bea and her diaper bag.

*

Outside the hotel, a few groups gather. More people are coming in than out. A light snow falls on the ground as we trudge single-file out of the hotel parking lot and down the sidewalk, through the adjacent residential streets.

"It doesn't have to be like this," John says, his voice straining. "We could try again."

I turn back to look at him, holding our daughter across his chest. I pull off my wig. It's covered in a thin layer of snow. "It's no fun anymore," I say. The words hang in the cold air, the unspeakable suspended momentarily between us.

When I reach the car, I can hear John's steps in the snow behind me. I look at the house we've parked in front of: hand-cut snowflakes taped to frosted panes. A Christmas tree lit up and framed perfectly in the front window. I can't decide if it's chintzy or wholesome. I hear John unlock the car, open the back door, and buckle Bea into her car seat.

"Shit," John says. "Shit. This can't be happening."

I keep looking at the house, serene and strangely devoid of people. *It's already happened,* I think.

"Mel," John says. " I lost my ring."

"What ring?"

"My wedding ring—it slipped off somehow. I think it rolled under the car."

I laugh, too loud, and the sound echoes down the empty street. I get in the passenger side, shut the door, drop the wig at my feet. The snow is falling heavier now. In the rearview mirror I see John on his hands and knees, frantically upturning snow that has browned with gravel and car oil.

I lean my head against the seat. My phone buzzes. An unknown Oregon number.

"Hi, Melanie? Hi. Sorry to bother—do you have a second?" My brother-in-law sounds like he's calling from the back room of a party.

"I have some bad news. Lacey's in the hospital. There was a suicide attempt—she's okay, but they want to keep her a few days. To figure out exactly what's going on."

Through the back window, I see my husband's silhouette bending over the car bumper. At first glance, he appears sick, the way his bare hands clutch the trunk, the tiny convulsions in his shoulders. But, his face obscured by the bumper, he could be anything.

"Jesus," I say finally. Silence for a moment, then the sound of what might be a firecracker over the line.

"How are the kids?" I ask.

"Blissfully unaware, thank god," says Walter.

"Thank god," I repeat.

"Only..." Walter hesitates. "They won't let them visit. They're worried it could aggravate her condition." *What condition*? I want to ask at first, but then I don't.

In the mirror, I see the *seifuku* girls, now draped in pastel coats rimmed with white fur, crowding around the back of our car. A girl wearing cat ears is bent over next to John; I can see her thigh, slick and glistening against the snow. One leans over the bumper, her back at a sharp right angle, another paws at the snow near the sidewalk. Muffled giggles edge in through the car windows.

"She's okay now. She's going to be okay," Walter continues. Outside the car I hear clapping and more laughter.

"I wish I could have been there," I say into the phone.

"There wasn't anything you could have done," Walter says distantly. "I'd better get back to the kiddos."

I look out the window and see the *seifuku* girls walking away, coats swaying off their hips, hands outstretched toward the snowfall.

*

"We found it," John says, holding up the silver band as he sits down in the driver's seat. He's sweating, and his face is red. He slides the ring onto his finger, holds it there.

"Did something happen?" he asks, eyes moving to the phone in my lap. I stare straight ahead, feeling many miles from home. John turns on the ignition, and heat floods the car. "It's my sister," I say. "She—"

Bea wails in the backseat, and I let her drown me out. John puts his hand on my thigh. He moves it away just as quickly. Snow accumulates on the windshield, darkens our faces. "I want to go home," I say, brushing aside the wig with my feet. The long strands spiral up my leg, a thousand snakes ascending.

From the Waist Down

We're in the hospital again, me and my wayward womb. My daughter, the birthday girl, was born four years ago. Once more, I wait and I watch the clock. The second hand slices through time—*sick, sick, sick*—a mean little knife. In a few hours, they will cut out a chunk of me, cut the whole damn thing out. This *thing* lies just below my belly button, swelling under the thin skin of my stomach. It's the size of a lime now. And it's growing.

Thinking about it makes me hysterical. Four years ago, to the day. At least Levi has help this time. My mom flew in from Sarasota. *Really*, she said. *I want to be there.* So, we decided to kill two birds with one stone: a birthday party and a surgical biopsy.

*

"They're here," Levi says brightly. He saunters into the hospital room, arms full of impeccably wrapped presents. "And your mom brought more gifts." My husband is relentlessly chipper. He sets the packages down, arranging them in neat piles under a shimmering banner: *Happy 4th Birthday, Nora!*

"Nora was hungry, so they stopped by the cafeteria," he continues, as he unties an oversized mermaid balloon from around his wrist.

"It's a little over the top, don't you think?" I gesture at the balloon. "And she's an hour late."

"C'mon, Ash, she's doing her best," he says, releasing the balloon to the ceiling.

The purple-haired mermaid bobs up and down with the

exhaust flow of the vent. She's shiny, with clear, unblemished skin, her taut stomach unmarked except for a pinprick of a belly button. No stitches or keloid scars. I want to tear her tiny body apart with my teeth.

When I sit up, the IV digs into my arm, so I lie prone against the hospital bed. Levi tapes a slew of unnaturally colored ocean animals to the beige walls. Party decorations overwhelm the small hospital room; when the nurse enters to check my vitals, she has to maneuver around the presents stacked precariously by the door-side table.

"Sorry," I say. "I guess my mom went a little overboard this year."

"That's what grandmas are for," the nurse chirps. She wraps the blood pressure cuff tight around my arm.

"It's her only grandchild," I say to the nurse, who smiles approvingly.

Everyone is doing what they're supposed to. The nurse nods and notes my blood pressure—"a touch too high, we'll keep an eye on it." The grandmother is overly doting, her concern manifesting in extra boxes and bigger balloons. The husband dutifully wrangles crêpe paper into little waves, assuming the role that should be mine, a faint suggestion of worry imprinted on his face. The only one off script is me. I'm growing a second uterus.

I had barely wanted the first one. Not after what it put me through four years ago. I know it's bad form and all, to disparage a perfectly good uterus, but I am so sick and tired of all this growing, growing, growing. I don't know if I'm allowed to say this, but I don't want to grow anything anymore.

*

In childbirth class, they tell you that pain is instructive. It lets you know something's wrong in your body. Unless you're giving

40

birth, of course—then, the pain is *productive*. That's actually what they tell you. Of course, it was a lie. I labored quite unproductively for thirty-six hours before they cut my stomach open, tore Nora out, left me only with that grim and smiling scar. Another untruth: that you'll be in so much pain during labor, you'll forget to be polite. That even the most timid of women becomes a lioness, feral and raging. They say you'll lose all sense of propriety. Not me. When I whined for an epidural, the attending nurse snapped, "Just breathe!" and that shut me up quick. She turned back to her computer while I waited for the anesthesiologist, crying mute tears, swollen and shallow-breathed. There was no heroic rage, no raw and powerful display. Whatever sound I made was a whimper turned inward.

*

By now, the IV has wedged itself deep into my forearm, nearing bone. The hospital bed is indifferent, and the machines encircling me beep and whirl on cue. I hear the rhythmic steps of hospital personnel in the hall, shadows passing under the door. The squeak of nurses' orthopedic footwear on linoleum floors. Clipboards clacking to rest on the backs of doors. All the natural cadences of the hospital. But the thing inside me continues to throb of its own accord.

Levi has finished the crêpe paper waves and is unrolling a life-sized mermaid poster. The mermaid is nothing from the waist down. All blank space.

"Is she on straight?" he asks, holding it against the wall.

"I don't think Nora likes mermaids," I say. Nora likes jellyfish—amorphous, clear, and fleshy. Mermaids must have been my mom's idea.

"You aren't even looking."

I wave my hand around theatrically at the four corners of the room. "Good job! Now you can't tell we're in a hospital—oh wait, never mind." I had meant to sound airy, but I just sound bitter. Levi frowns and says nothing.

"What time is it?" I smile because I feel guilty about my bad attitude.

"Almost noon," he says, still fiddling with the poster.

"Nora and my mom should be here by now. They'll be thrilled."

Levi starts rummaging through the brown paper bag of party supplies from my mom.

"They're coming to get me for surgery at one," I add.

He pulls out three long pins from a mesh bag. Metal pins with pearlized round tops, the kind old ladies use for sewing projects. They glint under the fluorescent lights. Punitive little things.

Levi laughs. "Jesus, are these to pin on the mermaid tails?"

I shrug. "Style over safety. That's my mom."

"I think we'll skip the party games," he says, carefully placing the needles back in the bag.

"Did I ever tell you how she'd dress me in a bikini and heels for the pool?"

"Well, you look good in heels."

"Levi, I was ten."

He squints at me, like he can't quite see my face. A phone vibrates on the table, and I feel the edges of the small room shake. "They're coming up," Levi says. "Do you need anything? Are you comfortable?"

I shake my head and smile like a wild thing.

*

But I need plenty. I need to know: what is this thing inside me? At my CT scan, with my veins lit up, burning with liquid neon solution, I caught a glimmer of it. In the center of my body, an abdominal mass, four centimeters long. At first, they thought it was cancer. Eventually, tests showed invasive uterine tissue. I had a strange desire to see an excised sample, behold it with my own eyes. I imagined it bloody and aching, like a newborn.

The thing inside me continues to pulse, a rhythmic pounding in time with the beeping of the machines, or maybe I'm just imagining it. Yeah, I'm a medical marvel: no one can tell me how this happened. Maybe the obstetrician didn't rinse out the abdominal cavity thoroughly after the c-section, allowing microscopic tissue to root into the fibers of my abdomen. Maybe I have some sort of rare disease that makes my uterus grow in places it shouldn't. Maybe it'll come back again. Maybe I won't. Maybe, maybe, maybe.

*

The hospital room door is cracked open. I hear Nora skipping down the hall. The soft soles of her shoes make a hollow sound, echoing after her.

"Slow down, Nora! Don't break anything." My mom sounds far away.

"Grandma, what's this?"

"That's a gurney."

"What's a gurney?"

"It's a bed with wheels."

"Can I sleep on it?"

"No, it's for sick people."

"Oh. Is that Mom's gurney?"

They enter the room. My mom carries a large, pink cake covered with candy shells and glittering sprinkles. Levi whisks Nora up, spins her around the room, dislodging a couple of stray balloons. Nora howls with delight. I stare at the snaking wires that tether me to the IV pole, too close to Nora's swinging feet.

"Happy birthday, big kid!" Levi says, releasing her to the floor.

"What's this?" Nora asks, pointing to the pin-the-tail poster.

"It's a mermaid, silly!" my mom says. "You love mermaids!"

"But where's her fish tail?" Nora's head tilts horizontal.

"It's a game—you close your eyes and try to pin the tail on. It's fun!"

"She looks weird like that," Nora says, taking a step back.

My mom chews her bottom lip into a smile, but says nothing. I think of those long, thin pins. I think of all the sharp and dangerous objects around us. How soft and fragile a body is.

*

When Nora was born, I felt for the first time the close proximity of my own death. I didn't see it right away. I failed to notice it looming over me, leering at my big, pregnant body as I dragged it into the Hospital of the Holy Cross, practically splitting at the seams with all of the life I was about to expunge.

I didn't notice it when I passed the statute of the Virgin Mary in the courtyard, cradling her miracle child, stoic and unsmiling. I was forty-three weeks along; my mom joked that Nora would have stayed inside me forever if I let her.

Seven days later, I left the hospital, hollowed out. The orderly wheeled me outside. I clutched my baby like a shell-shocked veteran grips their gun, scanning the horizon for nothing. The orderly droned on about car seats and legal liabilities, as he parked me next to an old woman waiting for the bus. She had yellow teeth and was smoking a stubby cigarette; she looked like she had been waiting outside for a very long time. The old woman glanced at me, then Nora, and said, "Oh, a fresh one! They smell nice when they're new." Her long, bony finger peeled back Nora's swaddling clothes. "Looks good enough to eat," she coughed, pinching my daughter's jaundiced cheek. As Levi drove up with the car, I pictured the operating room, bright and cold, the red glint of metal reflecting blood. Doctors counting in far-off voices. I knew then, my body didn't belong to me anymore. Something had been taken from me.

*

Nora creeps back up to the disembodied mermaid torso, which hovers just above the crest of a wave. The mermaid's placid smile is maddening.

"Dad, are mermaids monsters?" Nora asks.

"Not really," he says.

"Of course not, honey," my mom says. "They're very friendly."

"They're only pretend," I say.

A nurse pops her head in the door. "It's almost one—time for the main event," she says.

This is the nurse I like: the only one who doesn't hold it against me when I cry about old scars; who's never said, "at least the baby was healthy" or "all's well that ends well."

"I'll be back in a few minutes to prep you for surgery," she says. "This'll all be over soon."

She closes the door, it seems, in slow motion.

Nora is bouncing on a chair, reaching to pull a strand of streamers off the wall. She is unfazed by the nurses and their squeaky shoes, the machines with their infinite wires and red blinking lights. She looks over to Levi, face full of unrelenting joy and says, "Daddy! Look! Shine!" Taking a handful of glitter from the table, she throws it into the air. It rains down over everything, iridescent greens and blues against the beige of the room.

My mom clutches her neck and gasps, "Oh Nora! What a terrible mess!" Nora laughs unfettered as Levi looks around for a broom. I hold tight to the frame of the hospital bed as if the room is about to be swallowed whole.

*

"Okay, kiddo, Mom's getting ready for her big surgery. We can open up the rest of the presents at home." They nudge Nora in my direction. Her feet shuffle against the linoleum.

"Feel better soon, Mama." She picks at the glitter on the hospital blanket.

"Happy birthday, love bug."

She looks up at me. Her immense blue eyes aren't mine or my husband's. They are something else entirely. "Can I see it?" she asks, out of the corner of her mouth.

"See what?" At first, I think she means the large wrapped box Levi is struggling to fit into a grocery bag.

"The thing inside you."

I'm suddenly struck by a heavy feeling, a desire to shield my daughter from some nameless terror. My mom stands behind Nora, sharpening her nails with an emery board, honing the tips with sullen, deliberate strokes. She stares intently out the window at something in the distance. From my bedridden angle, it looks like nothing but empty sky.

"Can I see it?" Nora asks again. Her eyes are fixed on me.

"Sure, kiddo," I say as I pull up my hospital gown, revealing the papery skin of my stomach. The area under my belly button is circled in black ink, in preparation for surgery, branded with the surgeon's initials: *KM*. "See, it's just a weird little bump."

"Weird little bump," she says, singsong, to my stomach. "That's what it's called?"

"Well, it's called an abdominal mass, I guess. Maybe, a growth?"

"What's a growth?"

I shrug. "Just a thing that happens sometimes. I don't know why."

Nora's eyes narrow, two tiny blue pools ebbing.

Levi is stuffing used-up wrapping paper into a bag. "Are you sure you don't need me to stick around?" he asks. I glance at my mom, silent at the window, arms folded into her body as if nursing a wound.

"I'm fine," I say. "Don't worry about me."

Then I watch the three of them disappear out the hospital door, down the long hallway.

*

My therapist always tells me to listen to my body. *Where do you feel that anger? Where does your fear live?* I finally found it: it has crept into my core. And today they will cut it out entirely, carve away a piece of muscle with it, dissect this thing and name it. This *thing*: is it a piece of me, or isn't it? Did I—could I have—willed it into existence? All those bad thoughts balled up tight inside me, unresolved and left to fester.

Everyone agrees: this thing must go. Whatever I am growing is hideous. Freakish. Yet, as I sit here alone, surrounded by half-eaten cake and glitter settling into the folds of my hospital blanket, it occurs to me: this thing inside me is its own dark miracle. A tenderness and a violence—celebrating a birthday of its own. If I cradle my hand over it, I can almost feel it kicking.

Estate Sale

I awoke to the wind slamming against the shutters. I'd been dreaming about my father again. The night before, I learned he had lost his right eye. In my dream, I swallowed it. The soft, slick globe went down hard in my throat, sat heavy in my stomach.

This was the same morning my neighbor disappeared—the windiest in recent memory. From my window, I saw them selling off his paintings, hundreds of them. They laid his life's work across the front lawn, spread thinly on a green military-style tarp. Bargain hunters and well-wishers parked haphazardly on the street to rifle through the estate. They had to put rocks on the canvases to keep the wind from sweeping them away like feathers.

I put on my heavy coat and went out, stepping over dead branches that had fallen overnight. My neighbor to the left, Jeanine or maybe Jenny, stood in her fraying bathrobe at the road's edge, arms tucked tight across her chest. "Did you know Ron?" she asked without looking at me. I didn't. "He's a local celebrity. A real talented painter." She rocked back and forth on her heels. "Great guy, too."

"Is he dead?" I asked. I guess she didn't hear me; she never answered. My voice must've been drowned out by the wind.

"Fifteen dollars for an original Ronald Watts! What a shame." I left Maybe Jenny there rocking as I crossed the street to the house where Ronald Watts had lived.

The front door was open, and a smiling, sunny woman stood on the porch, holding a clipboard. She was dressed unseasonably in gauzy tights, a delicate and glimmering mesh. Through the door, I could see inside the entire house. The living room bled into the kitchen, a small cell of a bedroom on the right.

I lingered on the fringe of the lawn and listened to the smiling woman speak over her clipboard to a lady in a puffy, fur-trimmed coat.

"He came to the bank with an armful of paintings, wanted me to send them off to some gallery in Seattle. He thought I was his art dealer."

"Oh my god," the lady said, hand hovering over her mouth in perpetual alarm. "That poor man."

"And he kept withdrawing all this cash. He'd hand me a painting, then make a withdrawal. Multiple times a day. Like he was making a sale. That's when I knew something was seriously wrong."

"Jesus. Alzheimer's is a bitch."

"Yeah, he was in pretty bad shape. I asked around about any family. Eventually I found out he lived here alone. His daughter's in Alaska. When I called, she had no idea—no idea he was even sick."

The clipboard woman turned towards me, cheerfully encouraged me to go inside: there were more paintings there. I joined the crowd of strangers filing in and out, squeezing their bodies through a maze of piled-up frames, beating down what remained of the carpet. It felt illicit, like wandering through a crime scene. The only furniture was a battered office chair and a particle-board bookcase, both marked "FREE." I kept my hands in my pockets, careful not to touch anything.

I hovered in the living room, pretending to study the furniture, the unraveling edges of carpet. But I watched the two women on the porch through the filmy window. Their voices pierced me, blathering little alarm bells.

"His daughter wouldn't fly out here. Couldn't be bothered, right? I felt so bad, he's such a sweetheart. I had to do something, you know? I offered to organize this sale and raise money for his hospice care. His daughter said, sell everything."

"Alexis, that's awful!"

"Yeah, I wanted to shake her through the phone. Like, excuse me, ma'am, do you understand what I'm saying? Your father is very sick and he needs help!"

"Well. Thank God you stepped up."

"Oh, I love Ronnie. He's been nothing but a sweetheart to me. Every time he came into the bank—always smiling, asking me about school..."

"He's lucky he has you."

"It's nothing, really. If it were my dad, I'd want someone to do the same."

"Of course. *Of course*. Still, it's a shame..."

"It *is* a shame," I mutter to myself. "A goddamn shame what men do to their daughters." I begin to examine Ronald Watts's empty bookcase, its frame warped and sloping inwards. Somewhere, my own father sits in a small house like this. My father, with hands like broken branches, who leers with his one good eye. Is he expecting me?

Does he wonder who will take care of him as his memory fades and his grip weakens? Does he clutch at his memories in the growing dark, or is he grateful to lose them?

My father is very sick and he needs me.

My father. His eye a globe, containing the world, reflecting me back to myself. He was always looking at me. And all I ever wanted was to be seen.

*

Before I left the house of Ronald Watts, I bought a painting: a little girl sitting on the trunk of a tree that lies fallen across a pond. Bare feet dangle towards the dark water below. Her dress is coiled around her thighs, windswept, revealing the partial white of her panties. She is staring down at her reflection. Her awkward, slender body angles away from the viewer. Away from Ronald Watts.

"Does 10 dollars sound fair?" the young woman asked. I said nothing, just took the bill from my wallet and offered it up to her, watched it flap in the wind like a blind and flailing bird.

The New Jenny

Jenny Rench was 36 when she decided she needed a weapon. For protection, mostly.

She had been hiking alone down an unfamiliar trail, shadowy and poorly lit, though it was near noon. Nature towered above her: the Chuckanut Mountains, the Douglas firs. Birds shrieked in the distance. Her footsteps on still-thawing dirt. She was alone out here, and Jenny had never been good at being alone. No, she reminded herself, that was the *old* Jenny—the co-dependent, the enabler, the doormat Jenny. Today marked the first day in the bright and shining life of The New Jenny. Post-divorce Jenny. The Jenny who exercised and ate right, who didn't let men push her around, who sported a trendy-but-age-appropriate haircut. The Jenny who hiked alone in January on secluded trails. Brave Jenny.

The idea of a weapon came to her in the wilderness like an angel. It would save her from her old self. But, what sort of weapon? Jenny looked up and down the long stretch of trail. Bear mace? Pocket knife?

No, it needed to be a gun. Had to be. A gun meant business, like Jenny meant business. It demanded recognition.

Besides, everyone had a gun nowadays, even women—especially women, given the way things were trending. Jenny's yoga teacher, her childless aunt, her septuagenarian dog-sitter: all newly minted gun owners. Jenny imagined this brigade of armed women, stopping by the shooting range after the gym or before cocktails. Their pistols discreetly concealed in designer purses that brimmed with self-respect. These other women had found the secret short-cut to living fearlessly. Why not Jenny, too?

To start, Jenny didn't know beans about firearms. Her husband, Jack—former husband—was a pacificist and a vegetarian. He was the kind of guy about whom people said, "Oh, Jack? He wouldn't hurt a fly!" Jack hated guns. He hated them almost as much as he hated meat and, Jenny eventually learned, monogamy. *Stop feeling sorry for yourself. New Jenny, remember?* Jenny tried to focus on how a firearm might feel in the palm of her hand, the reassuring weight of it. Then, unbidden, Jack's face materialized: a look of surprise, mixed with a tinge of fear. Maybe, even, regret.

Jenny heard rapid footsteps behind her on the trail. A man in a neon running shirt and '80s-style headband jogged past her at an enviable clip. Jenny yelped in surprise. She could hear the indistinct blare from his headphones as he came close. He gave her a cool little nod in passing, which seemed to Jenny to be an apology—for startling her, perhaps, or in recognition of all the things he could do to her, how he might overpower her at the drop of a hat, were he that type of guy. And what could she have done, all alone out here, with nothing except her car keys, her soft and shapeless arms? Jenny noticed that Jogger Man looked a bit like Jack—tall, lanky, with just the right amount of muscle. Nearly twice her size.

Jogger Man would never expect someone like Jenny to have a gun. *Surprise, fucker,* she'd quip, snapping the pistol out of the cup of her bra. *Guess you got more than you bargained for.* She imagined that hangdog look, that feeling of helplessness, transferred from her to him. The delicious role reversal. *This has all been a misunderstanding!* he would blubber. *I got carried away. I'm so sorry Jenny, can you ever forgive me?* He might get down on his knees in the dirt and pine needles, bow his balding head, and beg for forgiveness. *You're the only one for me. I was a fool. I took you for granted, I sold you short, but I was so wrong. Give me another chance.* Then the new Jenny would smile sweetly while pulling the drenched sweatband up from his temples to gently place the pistol against his perspiring forehead. *Bam.*

*

Rainier Arms sat in the midst of a shitty strip mall off I-5, sandwiched between a day spa that never seemed to close and the shuttered office of Carma Parris, LSW, Marriage & Family Counseling. Jenny knew this parking lot well, having spent considerable time here crying in her car before and after couples therapy. At first, Jenny and Jack had planned to work things out, to save their marriage of seven years. This was before the girl got pregnant, at which point he said he had to do the right thing, which was to move in with her and their unborn baby. In two weeks' time, Jack had packed up his belongings, served Jenny divorce papers via private carrier, and blocked her on social media. They hadn't even made it to their third appointment with Carma Parris.

In the parking lot, Jenny smiled at herself in the rearview mirror. The blunt cut of her bob cast imposing lines against her cheeks, shadows at sharp angles. *Imagine what Jack would say, if he saw me here*, Jenny thought. She straightened her spine, steeling herself for her present purpose. The new Jenny can do hard things. The new Jenny will get out of her car and walk into that gun store like she owns the place. She brushed the stray fringe out of her eyes and went inside.

"Can I help you, ma'am?" The kid behind the glass counter's face had a glazed, sticky texture. Jenny moved through the store's single aisle towards him. "I want to buy a gun," she said.

"Alright, ma'am," the kid said, scratching a red spot on his neck.

"You don't have to call me ma'am. It's just Jenny."

The kid stared straight through Jenny as if she hadn't said

anything. Jenny continued, "I've never had a gun before."

"Alright," said the kid. "Intended use?"

"I'm sorry?"

"Concealed carry? Home defense? Competitive shooting?" He smiled, it seemed, at Jenny's expense.

"Oh. Self-defense. I like to hike by myself, so I thought..." She wondered where she was going with this. *My husband left me, I'm alone, and I need something to show that I'm okay.* But the kid had already crouched down and unlocked the display case, sliding the glass to one side and pulling out a slim, dark gun. He pushed it across the counter to Jenny.

"This'll be what you're wanting. Smith and Wesson M&P Shield. Plenty of power in a small package. Tons of safety features, too. "

"Oh," said Jenny, gauging its weight in the palm of her hand. "It's so light."

He beamed. "That's right, ma'am. 1.3 pounds, unloaded. It's our most popular model with women. User-friendly. Easy to handle. Not bad looking, neither."

Jenny nodded, her finger caressing the trigger. "It's beautiful."

"You've probably heard of it before, actually. It's the same gun Casey Miller used in the San Jose shooting."

"Oh," she said.

The kid looked at her, expecting more.

"I'll take it," Jenny said.

*

Those first days felt like a new beginning, like that silly rebirth they talk about in morning yoga class. *I am a force of nature,* thought Jenny. *For the first time, I'm in control of my life.* No more weeping in the bathroom during lunch breaks. Even her colleagues at the bank would say she seemed different. Glowing. Jenny would smile and shrug, as though she had no idea what they were talking about. But she would know she'd changed. She was no longer one of those boring, pliable women whose husbands left them for newer models. Instead, she was the type of woman who men *ran away from*. When she walked back to her car at the end of her shift, into the dark gloom of the parking lot, she would no longer grip her keys in her fist like a false hope. Instead, she would hold her head high, meet the darkness straight on. *Go ahead,* she'd taunt the purse-snatchers, the would-be rapists. *Come see what I'm capable of.*

But late at night, even the new Jenny couldn't fend off the intrusive memories of Jack. Weekend mornings when he would coax her awake with a cup of coffee. How he'd stare at her, as if trying to convince himself she was more beautiful with each passing year. Jenny tried to cajole their dog, Jericho, to climb up into bed with her, but he stayed parked by the door, expecting Jack to return any minute. This is when Jenny lost her resolve altogether and started scrolling through social media.

Even though Jack had blocked her, it was easy to find out that Sidney, the girl, was expecting any day now.

Jenny herself had never really wanted to be a mom—but she would have liked to have been asked. Jack never asked. Early on in their relationship, in their late twenties, they tacitly agreed parenthood wasn't for them. Only now, it seemed that maybe parenthood just wasn't for Jenny. She was too unsteady, too helpless herself to take care of someone else. Was that it? Or were some women simply more impregnatable than others?

Jenny had only met Sidney once, before she knew Jack was fucking her. Sidney was his personal trainer. Jenny hadn't been jealous, at first; hadn't thought there was anything to suspect, even though Sidney was pretty, with that girl-next-door sort of easy charm. Slick ponytail and yoga pants, slight as a needle. She had a dimple on the apple of her left cheek, which appeared whenever she smiled, which was often. But wouldn't-hurt-a-fly Jack was brotherly and polite with women. Plus, Sidney was so young, having just graduated from college. What could they possibly have in common?

Lying in their old bed, Jenny subjected herself to an endless feed of Jack and Sidney: at the beach, smiling and impossibly tan, then at the doctor's office, holding hands against the backdrop of an ultrasound screen, gray and blurry behind them. That photo held her gaze for so long that it dissolved into pixels, giving way to a terrible voice: *No one will ever love you that way.* It came from somewhere deep inside her, deep enough that all the mantras and affirmations in the world were powerless to silence it. *Poor, sad Jenny. Good-for-nothing Jenny.* The voice sounded like Jack. It became so loud, Jenny wanted to jump through the bedroom window, shatter the glass and feel the shards imbed themselves in her body. Tiny needles of pain: an outside to match the inside.

But, no—that was the old Jenny's routine. The old Jenny would self-flagellate, convert emotional pain into self-harm. *It's so adolescent,* Jack had said to her once, when she displayed the long, thin cut on the soft underside of her arm. *And, Jesus, Jenny, you hardly broke the skin.* Yes, she had been immature, dramatic, pathetically transparent. Even now, she felt the fresh swell of shame. To have treated herself as collateral damage. Just like Jack had, after all, just like so many other people. She was better than that. Deep down, she needed to believe she was better than that.

Jenny went to her bedroom closet and took the lockbox down from the top shelf. She entered the combination, and there sat her gun: a solid, grounding thing. She took it out and held it. It was so tiny, but when it spoke to her, its voice was deep and certain. *You are powerful,* it told her. *You are better than that.* She brought the gun into bed with her and, for once, didn't wake until morning.

Jenny woke with her gun on the pillow beside her, its metal exterior gleaming in the morning light. So small, yet so substantial. It sang to her: *You are in control. You can make him feel sorry.* All she needed was to see Jack one last time. She would show him she was better, that he had underestimated her.

It wasn't hard to find where he lived now. A friend of a friend of an ex-friend had posted gratuitous pictures of their housewarming party, their apartment complex, the number on the door. Forest Glen: that sprawling, moss-infested dump down by the university. It was mostly off-campus housing for college kids, alongside a fair share of low-grade drug dealers and feral cats. The kind of place the old Jenny was afraid of—too wild, too many strangers leering from weathered balconies. But the new Jenny waited until dark, then drove over to Forest Glen with her gun under the passenger seat. Once she'd parked in front of Jack's apartment, she retrieved it, nestling it into her coat pocket. It felt warm against her palm, a live beating heart. *Make him feel sorry*, it thrummed.

Jack would be back from work soon. She would wait until the dashboard clock read 7:00. She pictured the look on Jack's face as he walked in the door and saw Jenny, with her new haircut and new gun, sitting on the floor with his pregnant girlfriend, the two of them chatting away like conspirators. How desperately he'd wonder what they discussed—the things she could tell this girl! Jenny couldn't wait to see Jack squirm, watch the ticker tape of fear scroll across his face. After everything, Jack deserved to feel scared. Boy, would he be surprised to see the new Jenny.

*

Jenny knocked on the door of apartment C-6. At first, it seemed like no one was home, but eventually the door swung open, and there was Sidney, in a stretched-out shirtdress and stained yoga pants. She looked surprisingly dowdy for someone so young. Her hair was greasy, her skin covered in a thin sheen of sweat. White pimples crested her nose and chin. And she was very, very pregnant.

"Can I help you?" Sidney said groggily. She plucked the back of her shirt free from the elastic band of her pants.

"I'm looking for Jack Rench, is he here?"

Sidney's eyes widened in recognition. "He's not here," she said, moving to close the door before the words had left her mouth.

Jenny wedged her shoulder against the doorframe and pulled the gun from her coat pocket. Sidney stumbled backwards. "I really need to speak to him," Jenny insisted. "Just for a second—I can come inside and wait."

*

Jenny stood in the middle of a cramped, ill-equipped kitchen. Past the kitchen was a peeling leather couch facing a television, and beyond that an unmade bed flush against the back wall. The apartment was a studio; it had looked much bigger, and cleaner, in the pictures. Instead, the furniture—an assortment of particle board tables and empty bookshelves—seemed to cannibalize whatever space the apartment had originally offered. With her foot, Jenny shoved a bulging duffle bag out of her way. A hospital bag, readied for the birth. It bumped up against one of the unsteady tables, tipping it over and sending a cup of orange liquid oozing onto the carpet.

Jenny glanced down at the gun in her shaking hand. "I really need to speak to Jack," she said.

Sidney was gripping the back of the couch, breathing wildly, eyes darting from Jenny to the front door. "Oh my god," she said. "Oh my fucking god." Her legs buckled and she crumpled awkwardly, out of sight behind the couch. Jenny moved closer, keeping between Sidney and the door. Sidney cowered, folded in on herself, a bloated oblong ball.

Sidney let out a weak little moan. Tears rolled down her cheeks. Everything about her was round and swollen. Jenny hadn't meant to scare her, and she was sorry for that. *I could have been you,* Jenny thought. *I was you. Collateral.*

"Are you going to kill me?" Sidney asked, her voice breaking.

"Oh, god, no," Jenny said. "No. I'm here to see Jack."

"I told you, Jack's not here." Sidney broke into another long wail. The front of her shirt was wet.

"I'm sorry," was all Jenny could say. Suddenly, she felt very foolish. Where was the secret-sharing, the whispery girl talk? This particular girl was in no condition to chat. Jenny sat down on the arm of the couch, held the gun against her chest to steady her racing heart. She needed to think for a second. "I thought I'd surprise him," Jenny said, finally.

"Oh my god, oh my god..." Sidney started doing that weird, forced breathing Jenny had seen pregnant women do on TV. Sidney was sweating through her maternity shirt. Her chest glistened with splotchy red patches, scarlet tendrils reaching up her neck, blooming towards her face.

"Hey, no, it's okay." Jenny hopped off the couch and knelt beside Sidney. Sidney scooted back awkwardly on all fours, as far away from Jenny as the studio apartment would allow. Sidney's back was against the frame of the bed now, her feet near Jenny's. Jenny made a show of tucking the gun back in her coat, watched Sidney watch her. "I don't want to hurt you, Sidney. Okay?"

Sidney had both hands around her stomach, her face contorted like melted plastic. Jenny needed to calm the girl down somehow. Just until Jack arrived. Where the hell was he, anyway?

"Boy or girl?" Jenny asked.

Sidney looked at her, trembling.

"Your baby." Jenny smiled in a way that made her cheeks hurt. "Is it a boy or girl?"

"Girl," Sidney said quietly. She wiped her nose with her hand.

"Aw," said Jenny, because she couldn't think of anything else. This made Jenny laugh. "Guess I'm not much of a baby person."

Sidney let out a choking whimper and rocked back and forth again.

"I'd make a horrible mother, anyway," Jenny continued. "Too selfish. I don't want to share my body for nine months! Isn't that awful?" Jenny was nervous, rambling on about herself like this. "Who knows, maybe someday I'll adopt."

"I need to go to the bathroom," Sidney said.

"Oh," said Jenny, resisting the impulse to reflexively assent. She craned her neck to look around the couch. Next to the tiny kitchen was a door that was, presumably, the bathroom. And there lay Sidney's cell phone, face up and glowing on the nearby kitchen counter. "Maybe you can wait? Just until..."

"Please, I really have to."

"I'm sorry, but—" Jenny started, then corrected herself: *Stop apologizing*! "You can't. We have to stay put until Jack comes. What the hell is taking him so long?" She was starting to wonder if Jack was ever going to show up. Typical Jack. How long had Jenny been waiting for him to show up? How many wasted years? There had always been something else for Jack, and then eventually, someone else. She resented how, even in his absence, he always seemed to have the upper hand.

Sidney continued to wheeze. It was ten minutes to eight. That son of a bitch, if he had just been here like he should have... "You could go into labor at any minute!" Jenny said. "Where the hell is he?"

"I don't know. I'm sorry, I'm so sorry." Sidney cradled her head in her hands and moaned. Jenny noticed a wet puddle forming on the carpet beneath Sidney, the briny smell of urine.

"Don't," chided Jenny. "Don't say that. I've been sorry my whole life. You know what it got me? This." She gestured around the small apartment. "An ex-husband with a pregnant girlfriend. A dead-end job I've had for more years than I care to count. Superficial friends who've stopped calling, after..." Jenny trailed off. "You spend your whole life apologizing to people, bending over backwards, feeling so goddamn sorry all the time, and you think that it makes you a good person—a loveable person—but, I'm sorry, it doesn't."

Sidney sniffled, wide-eyed and wordless.

"Anyway," Jenny continued. "You don't have to apologize to me. Believe it or not, I'm over it. I mean, it's not like I don't have residual bad feelings—of course I do—but I have no regrets." Jenny took a deep breath, reassessing. "That's not quite true. I've been trying to be more honest with myself. I have tons of regrets: so many that I'm basically broke, between all the therapy and wine. But, deep down, I think it was for the best. It's so much better to know, you know?"

Jenny was aware of Sidney looking at her through her sticky strands of hair. The dimple surfaced on her cheek for a brief flash—a wince, perhaps a contraction. "What do you want from us?" Sidney finally mustered, though heaving sobs.

Jenny cringed at "us," which, of course, meant *them*. Not Jenny. She looked down and saw the gun in her right hand. She hadn't remembered taking it back out of her coat, but there it was, reassuring her of her purpose. "I want *him* to feel sorry."

Sidney tilted her head, as though sensing an opening, and leaned forward slightly towards Jenny. "You want him to feel sorry?"

"Yes. But not for this." Jenny gestured around the room. "For a lot more than this."

Through the thin apartment wall, two voices were shouting next door. *Fuck you asshole get out fuck you I live here too you're fucking psycho you know that?*

The voices stopped and an unbearable quiet descended. Sidney spoke again. "So you brought a gun—to get an apology?"

Jenny shook her head. "Not an apology. Not that kind of sorry. More like...a reckoning. *That* kind of sorry. Jack needs to see that I'm not the same person anymore—" She broke off, realizing her grip on the gun had reached the point of pain. "I'm not that needy, insecure, sad Jenny anymore. He was wrong about me. If he saw me now—really saw me—he would feel sorry."

"That does sound nice," Sidney said, with a thin smile as she slumped back against the bedframe. "But you know how Jack is. He might never show up."

Sidney looked worn down, defeated, but her eyes were soft and steady. There was something unshakable about that look, a quiet resolve. A knowing. And she was right, Jenny realized. Jack wasn't going to be frightened into some curative recognition of her. Sure, it would be comforting to believe that Jack, despite his mistakes, wasn't a bad guy. That he could look at Jenny and recognize her potential and her power, all those things that had been locked inside of her for so long. And, if he could see that, wouldn't that prove that he had loved her, in a way? But Jenny knew better now. He wasn't going to feel sorry. This was the new Jenny, but the same old Jack.

*

From the floor, Jenny watched the darkness skirt through the battered blinds of C-6. *Any minute*, she told herself, aiming her gun first at the closed door of the apartment, then the tall figure she imagined walking through it. Any minute now. She moved her aim down to the hospital bag and across the living room, to a shelf that held a few framed photos of Sidney and Jack, next to some Christmas cards. She imagined knocking each one down like the clown heads in one of those carnival games. *Bam. Bam. Bam.*

Pregnant Sidney was making all sorts of weird, strained noises. The color had left her face, and her head kept hitting the wall, sending tiny vibrations through the room as she rocked herself back and forth. That was when Jenny saw the new liquid, darker, pooling underneath Sidney. Blood soaking through her yoga pants and into the gray-green carpet. Had Jenny—? No, she convinced herself, no—her finger never touched the trigger.

Jenny felt brave as she dialed 911, brave as she sat with Sidney, covered in blood and amniotic fluid, holding her through contractions until the paramedics arrived. "I'm so sorry—" Jenny tried to say as they wheeled Sidney out on a stretcher, but she knew Sidney hadn't heard.

The new Jenny sat alone on the floor of the studio apartment, cradling her gun like a newborn. She listened to the sirens fade out, then in again, and waited for Jack to come home.

A Safe Haven for Writers

The whole place was empty.

But it wasn't really empty. Because here in the Overlook things just went on and on. Here in the Overlook all times were one.

—Stephen King, *The Shining*

Salt House is not as I expected. My resolve wanes as I drive my rental down the narrowing, gravel driveway—eroding with each abandoned car I pass, every piece of rusted machinery.

It doesn't look anything like the brochure. The pristine white farmhouse against the green Oregon forest crumbles before me. Chipped-up and covered in moss, browning, dissolving into its wild surroundings.

With no discernable parking, I stop on an expanse of spotty grass that must have been, at one point, the front lawn. The garage is a gaping mouth, revealing yellowed appliances and moldy boxes. Upstairs, a window sags under the weight of the years. I can hardly believe I'm in the right place, even as I read the sign's peeling paint:

Salt House
A safe haven for writers

I drove five hours to get here, five hours outside my comfort zone. This trip is supposed to be my metamorphosis, my odyssey, my chance to prove to my husband that I am still an independent woman who can get by on her own, at least some of the time.

This is where I will be staying. One week. Alone.

I step out of the car. A man stands at the side of the house, partially obscured by overgrown bushes. His hair is pulled back in a silvery ponytail, flannel shirt grass-stained and muddy. He watches. With one hand, I wave; with the other, I finger the canister of pepper spray packed in my jacket pocket only as an insurance policy: superfluous, but comforting. I had expected solitude.

"Is this an okay place to park?" I ask. "This is Salt House, right?"

He stares at me.

"It's my first time," I say to fill the silence.

The man raises both hands, a gesture of surrender. "I help Paul. He's the caretaker." His hands stay that way, suspended in the air, tremoring slightly. "*He's* the caretaker," the man says again, tilting his head to behind the house. The sound of a chainsaw flares.

He remains at the side of the house, arms lifted, eyes never leaving mine. I look back towards my car, briefly consider an escape. Instead, I walk towards the front door. Everything is fine, I reassure myself. This is fine.

The door is unlocked. Once inside, my spirits lift a little. The interior is charming: worn wood floors and built-in bookshelves, a white clay fireplace embedded in the center of the living room. The south-facing side of the house is all windows—walls of glass in the kitchen, the living room, the mudroom leading to the bathroom. The windows look out over a large meadow: ten acres of farmland that give way to wilderness against the Clackamas River.

Hazy smoke rises above the trees. It's wildfire season, even now in early October, the sky tinged pink like the first drops of blood.

I unpack and, unsure of what to do next, drift from room to room. It is common knowledge that writing residencies can be an adjustment, mentally speaking; the isolation crazymaking. *I'm not worried about solitude*, I'd joked with my husband. *It's people I can't stand.*

I recall the look on his face, a look I've grown accustomed to in recent years: his straight-lined mouth as he digests my stale joke, the wells of his eyes signaling his patience has been whittled away. It is his couples therapy face when he says, *I feel like her caretaker*. His solemn nod as our therapist speaks of *separate interior lives*. So, here I am, cultivating something of my own, many miles away from my house and my husband, in the woods outside Portland, listening to the Steller's jays shriek, wandering through a drafty old house like a phantom.

*

I follow the stairs as they curve to a second-story bedroom, mine for the next week. Two large windows admit an expanse of light, which illuminates the dust swirling mid-air with the frenzy of a million flying insects. The first window, by the writing desk, over-looks the meadow, where I see another man, perhaps in his late fif-ties, standing in the tall grass holding a machete. He runs a file up the length of the blade, sharpening it, the sound of each deliberate stroke ringing across the meadow. Paul, the caretaker. I watch him kneel down. He raises the machete above his head and it comes down with a thud. He continues this way, in circles, hacking at the grass.

I look away and notice a second window, beside my bed. It is awkwardly positioned, peering across the house and into another room that sits above the attached garage. This room is so close that I could climb out onto the roof and back in through its open win-dow. I see a slice of its interior at an angle: an oversized computer monitor, an acoustic guitar, hippie beaded curtains in the back of a self-contained apartment. Its tenant appears to be something of a movie buff. The walls are lined with vintage posters: *A Clockwork Orange*, *Lolita*, *The Shining*.

I unpack my clothes under the sideward gaze of Jack Nicholson. I'm reminded that *The Shining* is the story of a guy who becomes unhinged during a writing residency and tries to murder his wife and child on account of writer's block. This realization is oddly comforting. Even if I have difficulty adjusting, I can pretty much guarantee I won't murder anyone. I'm not crazy; *he's* crazy.

I call my husband as the sun sets over the meadow.

"How is it?" Grahame asks.

"It's—" I watch Paul through the window as he traipses towards a dilapidated barn. "It's fine. A little weird. The house is pretty old."

"Uh-huh."

"There's a lot of bugs, and the doors don't really shut properly, and—" I lower my voice. "And there's this guy. I haven't talked to him yet. But he's just...around."

"What kind of guy?" Grahame asks.

"The caretaker. The brochure mentioned an on-site caretaker, but I didn't think he'd be living in the same house. I can see straight into his room from my window."

"That does seem a little weird," Grahame says. "Kind of like one of your stories."

"The worst part," I continue, "is there are no curtains, anywhere. None. I feel completely exposed."

"Well, I'm glad you're giving it a chance," he says. "Proud of you." His words are clipped off, a signal that there is nothing else to say.

I go to bed as soon as it's dark. I can't bear to sit in the lit-up house, looking out into the blackness of the meadow, unable to see what's staring back.

*

The next morning, I awake at dawn to the sound of a rooster crowing in the distance. I slink downstairs to the bathroom, along the windowed corridor. I hear Paul's steps above me. My bathroom must be directly below his studio. I hear him urinating in sync with me. Is this strange? Both of us awake at the same time? Maybe I'd woken him up. I step across the cool, stone floor as lightly as I can.

I go to the kitchen table and take out my notebook. I am planning to write a piece for my book, a collection of domestic horror stories. Stories of what's just beneath the surface. The slick white SUV circling a suburban block, the stay-at-home mother with a sly smile and secret scar. But I can't write. I can't focus. I can hear Paul behind the house, and the whir of some nameless, ancient machine. Maybe I'll write a re-telling of *The Shining* with a female Jack Torrance. Only, she has no children to murder, and her husband has his own job, so she only has herself to haunt.

I consider going for a walk, but I don't want to run into Paul. We still haven't introduced ourselves. The longer this goes on, the more I dread it. So, I resume wandering the house, searching for inspiration, looking for ghosts. I study a stately bronze bust that sits prominently in the entryway. It's a sculpture by a local artist of an aging and shiny Leonard Salt, namesake of Salt House. A memoirist who wrote of his life during the Great Depression, Leonard published his first book, *Nirvana in a Nutshell,* at 81—to great, albeit regional, acclaim. The house belonged to Salt and his much younger wife, Ines. After she died, it was turned into this writer's retreat.

For the rest of the day, I conduct a thorough inspection of the home and its artifacts, hoping to learn about the people who lived here before. It's better than sitting at the kitchen table, unable to write and watching Paul ferry his tools back and forth across the meadow in a wheelbarrow. I read the spines on the living room bookshelves: *Oregon Poets, American Pastoral, Complete Illustrated Kama Sutra*. Five DVD copies of *American Pie*—one opened, four still in shrink wrap. Propped on the top of one shelf is a portrait of an old woman sitting on a blue couch. Ines. Next to her picture is another canvas, an oil painting of this very room. There's the blue couch, the bookshelf, the wall of windows. We do not see what is outside the windows, it is all gray. There are oil paintings in every room, I realize later. None are hung: they sit propped against walls, on the floor, or atop dressers and tables. Dozens of them, often depicting the exact room in which they've been placed. The artist never signed their work. Was it Ines? Had to be.

In the dying light of the bedroom, I study a framed poster hanging over my bed—the only picture in the house that is actually up on a wall. A grayscale photo of Leonard, in his nineties, wearing a woman's white-lace nightgown and posed suggestively on a marble staircase. "Take an Author to Bed," reads the poster's punchline. In the billowy gown, he looks swallowed up, childlike. One weathered hand clutches the banister, the other cradles a pile of books, including *Nirvana in a Nutshell*. He smirks at the camera.

I drift to sleep, only to be woken by voices. *Say it: you're a dirty whore*. It is a man's voice, heavy, like footfalls on gravel. My room is bright for the middle of the night. The hunter's moon. The sound of a woman's moaning follows through the bedside window. *I'm a dirty, dirty whore,* she admits, dreamily. I sit up in bed and crane my neck to look into the neighboring studio. I can't see Paul, but I see the display on the large monitor: a woman in pigtails and a pleated skirt, lifted above her waist. A man stands over her. *What's my name?* he demands. The woman shrieks. *What's my name? Daddy. Say it again. Daddy. I'm...a dirty little whore, daddy. Good girl.* The words become meaningless, devolve into guttural curses. I close my eyes, shivering, wrapped up in someone else's blankets.

The next morning, I am too tired to write. In the living room, I find a stack of newsletters in a desk drawer. *Dispatches of the Salt Society: dedicated to preserving the legacy and writing of Leonard Salt.* One issue's cover features a photo of a dozen men—the Salt Society—all old, white, and nearly indistinguishable from one another, standing in front of Salt House. They brandish gardening tools like weapons. Another issue includes an *in memoriam* to Ines: "Anyone close to Lenny knew his sweet, shy Ines—part of the furniture here at Salt House. She'll be missed." There is a recurring section, "A Pinch of Salt," that shares excerpts of Salt's unpublished writings. "Canoodling with Cannibals" in one issue; in another, a digression on "Labial Kissing Technique." There are full-page testimonials from previous recipients of the residency, accompanied by large, color photos. A wunderkind playwright from Duluth reclines on a riverbank in a bikini and sunglasses. Each newsletter ends with a call for new applicants: "YOUNG ARTISTS, ESPECIALLY."

A laminated "Free Copies" placard draws my attention towards a bookshelf devoted to Salt's own work. I avoid *Nirvana in a Nutshell,* with its drab Great Depression narrative, and pick up the thickest of his three books, *Hulda's Gift.* From the dust jacket cover: *An autobiographical triumph,* Hulda's Gift *is the story of Salt's life in the Columbia River basin, after settling there at age forty with his wife Hulda and their infant son. Salt is captivated by his wife's teenage niece, and must wrestle with his longing, as well as his loyalty to Hulda. In the end, he comes to an unusual realization and life-changing compromise. With brutal honesty and vulnerability, Salt recounts the past with an unblinking pen, to the delight and titillation of readers.*

His wife's teenage niece? I sit there all morning with *Hulda's Gift* in my lap, reading through the pristine copy. It begins when

Ines is twelve and first attracts the attention of her uncle. Salt describes her as a shy but pretty girl who would look at him through long, startled lashes. Her inability to speak without stuttering, which brands her as "slow" among family, further endears her to Leonard. Ines is at first resistant to Leonard's advances, but eventually capitulates after three resolve-chipping years. Wracked with guilt, Leonard wrestles with his ongoing affair for two more years before telling his wife. Hulda dies of an ironic blood clot in the heart soon after. Hence the book's title: Hulda's death is the gift that sets niece and uncle free. Free to marry and settle down together, building the house in which I now sit.

*

That night, I call Grahame from the backroom upstairs, the furthest place in the house from Paul's quarters. It is cramped. A bulky wooden easel stands in the middle of the room, and stacks of painted canvases line its perimeter, propped against the walls, piling on the floor, pouring out of cardboard boxes. More depictions of the house's rooms, from various angles, in various hues. A few empty landscapes. A nude sketch. The refinement in the technique over the years is apparent, a clarity and confidence emerging.

I wear a blanket over my shoulders. It is an unseasonably warm late October, 85 degrees and sunny every day, but this house does not let heat in. I feel like an old woman, hunched and shrouded.

"How is it?" Grahame asks, in a chipper way that presumes a specific answer.

"It's fine," I whisper into the phone as I watch a wasp hit against the windowpane.

"What's wrong?" His tone changes. I can sense his disappointment. To be this woman, always the cause of worry.

"The house is infested. There are bugs everywhere."

"That seems like something you wouldn't like very much." He

is weighing responses, leaving most unsaid.

"And I still haven't spoken to the caretaker—but he's always around, hacking up bushes or whatever."

"You should probably introduce yourself," he says.

"Yeah. It's been three days, so—" I pause. "Last night...I could hear him, in his room. I could hear what he was watching. It woke me up. He's always here, and like I said, there are no curtains, so the sound travels."

"Well," Grahame starts, taking a measured breath. "It seems like something you wouldn't like." I can tell he is holding back, but the subtext is: *It doesn't sound so bad.* The subtext is: *You're catastrophizing.*

I spare him the sordid details of what exactly I heard from Paul's room last night. That there are no locks on any of the doors. Or that the gate I'd been given a combination for prior to my visit...there was no gate. I don't mention that I've taken to walking around in the dark to avoid drawing attention to myself. That I'm in the dark even now, huddled in a closet, shivering and muttering into the phone. I withhold these things because I can already hear his disappointment.

"I'm glad you're making the best of it," Grahame says eventually. I don't mention my writing, and he doesn't ask.

"I am. You don't have to worry about me—not that you were."

"Why do you say stuff like that? Of course I'm worried about you."

"I didn't mean—no, I know. You didn't say you were worried, and I thought maybe we were pretending that you weren't. I know you are. But you don't need to be. I'm good."

"Maybe go for a walk tomorrow or something? Get out of the house, clear your head. When we talk tomorrow, I bet you'll feel better."

I awake again to the rooster. He seems so far away, but the sound carries. I wonder whether Paul could hear my conversation with Grahame last night. I creep down to the living room with his footsteps above me.

I return to *Hulda's Gift*. Leonard describes telling his first wife, Hulda, of his years-long affair with her niece. It is night. Hulda is in the kitchen, slicing potatoes into a cast iron pot. He feels afraid: this is the hardest thing he has ever done. He speaks so quietly, Hulda does not hear him at first. When she finally understands, she howls, curses him, runs to the bedroom and locks the door. But after some time, she invites him in. She is lying in bed, covers pulled up, back to him. He can hear her crying. He wants to comfort her, to touch her, but he knows better. She quiets herself.

The first thing she asks is: how long? He tells the truth. Two years. She screams as if her flesh were being torn off. "How could you?" she asks. He assures Hulda that he still loves her, wishes she had agreed to move away from Oregon years ago, when he had first asked, before it was too late. If only, if only. Hulda is silent, lies there as though in her coffin. The two of them stay like that, for an eternity, until she wraps herself around him. In the morning, she says she will forgive him. She must take responsibility for her own role in the ordeal. For allowing Leonard and Ines time together, for not suspecting. Three months later, Hulda is dead.

I find myself seething as I read this. Why do I care? Because I sit here trapped in this man's house. I read his great love story, and through the cracks in the retelling, I can see slices of myself, hidden and simmering. In his broken-down house that I am doomed to inhabit, my unwritten stories floundering in the dark.

*

That afternoon, back at my window, I wait until Paul disappears into the barn. *Get out of the house. Clear your head.* I pocket my pepper spray and hurry outside before he can reemerge. I walk through the meadow, past plowed, empty fields and into a dense forest with surprisingly well-kept trails. They lead eventually to the Clackamas. I find the river unnerving, its power drowning out all other sound. I continually look back to make sure I'm not being followed. The brochure mentioned that Salt House lies on private property, so any evidence of trespassers should be reported. But I'm alone. I sit on the bank. Across the river is a sheer cliffside that gives the impression that I've reached the end of something. I can't go any further; I can only go back.

A water snake languishes on the river's surface, its forked tongue darting wildly. I lean in closer, and it swims underneath the water, the neon green strip on its back revealing its hiding place. The rocks on the riverbed are pockmarked. I start sifting through them, looking for hag stones—rocks with naturally occurring holes through them. Legend has it that you can look through the hole and see the future. I spend the afternoon like that, turning stones over again and again, but I can't find any. The best I can do is one with an indent deep enough to fit my thumb in. I put it in my pocket with the pepper spray. It feels fitting: a stone with an almost-hole, the quality of almost-seeing, like walking through an unfamiliar house in the full moon's light.

I walk back through the woods towards Salt House. Everything is quiet but the leaves under my feet and a motor in the far distance. I lift my head and am startled to see a large wooden structure nestled among the firs—some kind of treehouse or playground. I creep towards it. The wood planks are clean, newer-looking, but everything else is covered by a thin layer of moss and leaves. The structure's central feature is a hanging platform, suspended in the air by chains. On the platform is a bare, cardboard-thin mattress. It is dark blue, with planets and rocket ships. A child's mattress. There are ropes and rusted clamps beside the platform. An abundance of lawn chairs are arranged in a semicircle. Discarded beyond the chairs are corroded shovels, plastic jugs filled with dull liquid, a stainless-steel basin. What is this place? I have no way of telling the age of things out here. Had Leonard come here with Ines? These signs of life might have been from decades ago or yesterday. I step on a rusted trowel half buried in the dirt and think back to the photo of the Salt Society, imagine those men tending this strange soil. Paul with his machete. I flee the scene as quickly as I can.

The trees recede, and Salt House emerges into view. I am half-running across the meadow when a voice cuts from somewhere in the sky.

"Hey! Stop! Hey!"

I startle and see Paul above me, kneeling on the barn roof, holding a hammer mid-swing. His shirt is soaked with sweat, a pile of shingles next to him. He crawls down the eaves, closer to me, stopping his descent at the roof's edge. I raise my hand to shield my eyes from the sun that looms menacingly behind him. He looks down on me, but I can't see his expression through the glare. "Sorry about the shouting," he says. "Been trying to talk to you all week, but you're a squirrelly one." He sets down the hammer but doesn't come down from the roof. Instead, he leans back on the incline. "View sure is nice up here." He pats the spot beside him, waits a beat, then smirks, or grimaces—I can't tell which. "Wanted to ask how you're holding up," he continues. "Is everything as you expected?" I shift on my feet. What is he getting at? The house? Had he overheard my complaints to Grahame? The platform in the woods? He must sense I've seen it. I search his face for an indication, but all I see are shadows.

"Yes," I say. "It is what I expected." He tilts his head in amusement, or perhaps anger.

"Good talking," he says, as though I'm the one not living up to expectations. I wave and hurry towards the house, through the front door, reaching back for the lock before remembering it doesn't exist.

That night, I tell Grahame the saga of Leonard and Ines.

"His wife—she was his niece! She was fifteen when they first slept together, then they got married, and she spent her whole life here. This guy writes openly about perpetrating abuse, and they give him a book deal for his unflinching honesty. It reads like a how-to manual. And this was the '90s. Didn't we know back then that you shouldn't sleep with your niece? When was that ever okay?"

"It's a great idea for a story," Grahame says.

"It's real life. And it's so shitty. This guy gets to write what happened. All the other characters become whatever he says they are. Ines lived here too! She existed, and we'll never know what she *actually* felt. Meanwhile, he lives forever as the author of a transcendent love story. But—God, she was fifteen."

"Yikes," says Grahame.

"And then, there's his first wife. The Hulda of *Hulda's Gift*—her gift was that she died."

"That is odd," Grahame says, conclusively.

"So, I finally met the caretaker today. He asked if I was okay. If the house was as I expected."

Grahame says nothing.

"Isn't that a weird way to phrase it? Wouldn't you ask, like, do you have everything you need?"

"I don't see what you're getting at."

I whisper into the phone. "He can hear me. He heard what I told you last night."

"Huh. Seems unlikely."

"How would you know? I'm telling you, sound travels here. I always hear him walking around the house, and the windows literally do not shut. I have no privacy. I can hear him above me when I'm in the bathroom, for chrissakes."

"That sounds like it would be uncomfortable for you," Grahame says. "But this is a residency, right? Other people have been there before. If privacy were an issue, I'm sure someone would have said something."

"What if they didn't? What if they were afraid to? What if I'm right, and there's something terrible going on?"

"What do you mean 'something terrible'?" Grahame asks.

I think of the child's mattress. The Salt Society. The picture of the playwright from Duluth, her eyes shielded by her sunglasses. Ines's paintings, never signed. I say nothing.

"You see the sinister in everything," Grahame continues. "Not everything is a horror story. Not everything is some awful conspiracy. The problem is your perspective. God, your negativity is *exhausting*."

I hear him regain his composure, return to his measured breath. "You can leave whenever you want," he says eventually. "Nobody's keeping you there."

I laugh. Because I understand one thing clearly: if I leave now, it will be the end of my marriage. I will be written off. A woman who can't take care of herself.

"What's the joke?" Grahame asks, his weariness seeping through each syllable.

"Nothing. You're probably right. If it were that bad, someone would have said something."

This seems to satisfy him. "So, how is the writing?" he resumes.

"Great," I lie.

*

The next morning passes, and the next, and the next. I watch from my window as the caretaker attempts to beat back nature. To prevent the house and its grounds from being swallowed up by wilderness.

I'm still not writing. It's this house: the pictures of Leonard and Ines, the newsletters proclaiming their great love. This house is a monument to wordless suffering, to dominant narratives, to a certain kind of truth-telling that silences what it does not speak. One man's love story is another woman's trauma.

In the middle of the night, I hear a voice seep through the walls of the house, catching just under the floorboards. I wasn't sure at first, in this house full of pretext and noise, but now I know. It is Ines. She's still here. And she reminds me why I can't leave yet either. Just two more days.

*

I want to finish this story. I just need to find the right perspective. I need to see clearly.

My final night, I take my notebook and walk back down to the banks of the Clackamas. I reach a bluff that overlooks a bend in the river. I've read about this place: it is where Leonard finally culminates his long seduction of Ines, on a camping trip. Leonard writes of how he ventures out in the middle of the night, crawls to Ines's tent, calls to her. The rushing river assuages his fear that anyone might hear him as he whispers through the fabric of her tent. When pleading doesn't work, he threatens to wake Hulda, get them both in trouble. Slowly, Ines unzips the tent and steps out, barefoot in a flowing, gossamer nightgown. Leonard embraces her and takes her hand, leads her further down the river bed. She trips on the stones. He can tell she is nervous by the way she holds back, by the way he must pull her by the arm through the moonlight. Once they are far enough from the tent, he draws her into another embrace. She is shaking, she cannot speak. He tells her not to be nervous, there is nothing to worry about. He asks her to remove her gown and she shakes her head. He removes it himself. Then he lays her down on the ground and takes her. Afterwards, he is elated. He is in love. He is a complicated man. But what of Ines?

I may have some idea. I sit on the beach, shivering in the middle of the night with my notebook: *Salt House is not as I expected*...I write, and I wait for a sign. All I hear is the empty forest, the river rushing by like tears, as the full moon looks on, unconcerned.

Thumb Stump

The balled
Pulp of your heart
Confronts its small
Mill of silence

How you jump—
Trepanned veteran,
Dirty girl,
Thumb stump.

—Sylvia Plath, "Cut"

Emilia Ann Carter was born the same night the president of the United States shot himself in the head. When the baby's mother, Polly, heard the news a full week later, she only felt as though she had stepped out of some long, languid dream. Emerging from the maternity ward clutching her newborn baby, she recognized everything in the world had changed. There was life before the hospital and life after, when the president was dead and she would forever be known as somebody's mother.

*

The birth itself had been a violent and bloody affair. After seventeen hours of blurry, hysterical contractions, the obstetrician put her hands inside Polly's failing cavity and relayed that the baby was in brow position. That is, eyebrows first, the baby's neck extended down the birth canal, instead of its chin tucked in, crown pointed towards its hoped-for escape. As such, the obstetrician informed Polly, vaginal delivery would be inconceivable. Polly's body was rolled into the OR for an emergency c-section, which Polly experienced as a waking autopsy. She thought she had died on the operating table. Afterwards, she couldn't explain this continued conviction that her body was a shattered, glasslike object, and not the malleable lump of flesh her rational mind knew it to be.

After, Polly was repeatedly advised by family and well-wishers to refrain from retelling such grisly details, seeing as the baby was born perfectly well (with ten fingers and as many toes, her aunt continually reminded her). To complain of a healthy baby was simply to invite disaster into one's life.

*

As the damage to her stomach was quite extensive and reluctant to heal, Polly had remained in the hospital with her newborn for seven days. With little to do but nurse, days passed slowly, sullenly. Golden streaks of colostrum congealed on sterile, white sheets, like slips from a leaky ink pen. Polly tried hard not to think about her body: cut and tender to the core, full of gauze, inert on the stiff hospital bed. Instead, she watched the baby, whose face was folded up and vaguely gelatinous. The baby wore a pair of thick, green mittens to keep from inadvertently scratching her delicate skin, giving her a turgid, amphibious appearance.

Little polliwog. Like her father called her as a child.

Little polliwog. Little pilgrim. My Polly. Her father had named her many things as a child, like a frenzied Adam blithely bestowing monikers upon the creations surrounding him. He peopled their private interior with his cryptic mythologies.

There was the *Homunculus.* His pet name for her left thumb, cut short by nearly half an inch compared to her right. It was squat and slightly bulbous at the top, with a short, wide nail bed. Her

grandmother had once called it a "murderer's thumb" as she murmured prayers under her breath and bemoaned the base-born
blood from the mother's side. Her father—a man of science, not
superstition—had christened it the Homunculus. *Little polliwog
and the Homunculus.* His low voice creeping over her bed: *You are
beautiful, no matter what.* And he would silently take her thumb
in his mouth and suck on it, slick tongue probing the ridge of nail,
teeth lightly resting on knuckle.

Polly adjusted the bundle on her chest. As she bent her left
wrist, the IV probed sharply against her bones. Her hands were
cold, her knuckles throbbed. At once, she noticed her left thumb,
suddenly unremarkable. She held it up to the right. They were
symmetrical: slender and inviting. Twin nail beds, equally pink,
equally spacious. She felt a sinking hole, an endless mouth of grief
centered in her chest, in that space now occupied by the newborn.
The clubbed thumb was no more.

*

On Wednesday afternoon, Polly's sister Lillian arrived at the ward.
The baby was sleeping in the bassinet as Polly spoon-fed herself
cold pasta from the hospital tray. Lillian sat in the room's only
chair, positioned in the far corner by an industrial-grade breast
pump. On the wall behind her was the pain scale chart, cartoon
faces aping the spectrum of human discomfort.

Polly punctured a hole in her box of prune juice. "Do you
remember my weird thumb?"

Lillian shifted in her seat, folding her arms across her chest.
"The toe thumb?"

"Yeah. It's the weirdest thing. I noticed yesterday, it's gone."

"What do you mean, *gone?*"

"I mean, it changed...It's completely normal, like the other
one. Look—" she held up both thumbs side by side—delicate

85

mirror images.

Lillian uncrossed her arms but didn't budge from the chair.

"Look!" Polly persisted.

Lillian sighed and pushed herself up. At the bed, she held both of Polly's hands noncommittally in her own. Slowly, she lowered them. "You got surgery?"

"No. It just happened. I noticed it yesterday."

Lillian shrugged. "Pregnancy is strange."

"But the bone...how could it just grow like that?"

"After what you've been through, growing out a thumb's nothing." Lillian moved back to the chair and sat down. "Did you tell the doctor?"

"No, why would I?" Polly threw the crumpled juice box back on the tray. "It doesn't matter anyway."

Lillian frowned. "Do you miss it?"

"I barely even thought about it. But it is a little unnerving."

"What's unnerving?"

Polly hesitated.

"It's genetic, right?" Lillian continued. "Does Emilia have it?"

Polly looked down at the baby in the bassinet, fingers obscured by green mittens. She said quietly, "I haven't checked."

"Oh. Well, you definitely would have noticed."

"Like I said, it's not something I think about—"

"You would have *noticed*."

Both women regarded the sleeping infant between them. Neither moved.

*

On Saturday, Polly's discharge paperwork was approved and she was allowed to leave the hospital. The cab driver helped her out of her wheelchair and into the idling car. He would not help strap in the baby's car seat—liability reasons, he explained. Polly bent over the car seat to secure the middle buckle herself, and the three of them proceeded onto the interstate. Polly looked at the sleeping baby, and then beyond, through the window on the other side of the cab. She watched the city skyline bleed by as they moved towards the outskirts, with their barren parking lots and aging fast food chains. A cramped-lettered sign outside a darkened strip club read, "Closed for good. Thanks for the memories."

*

At home, Polly fed the baby again and laid down on her bed. She turned on the news and fell asleep to the thrum of conspiracy theories and pleas for gun control in the wake of the president's passing. Some time later, the baby awoke, hungry. Polly rolled over, peering into the bassinet. The baby's face seemed too small to contain the mouth that gaped back at her.

Polly muted the television. She picked up the baby, arranging her on a nursing pillow and bringing her to her breast. The red mouth latched and was mercifully silent. Polly leaned back against the headboard. The baby pawed her froggy green fists at the breast. Somewhere in her head, a nurse chided Polly: *She needs tactile stimulation. She needs to use her fingers to explore her new world.* Polly peeled off the mittens, one after the other. The baby's hands moved, delicate fists curling and uncurling. Polly held out her pinky and felt the baby's tiny grip surround it with surprising sturdiness. *You are beautiful, no matter what.* Polly rolled her pinky over, studying the fingers that clutched. One, two, three, four…

And there it was, bordering its four upright counterparts: a small homunculus. A blunt, thick thumb much like her own had once been. A puckered face with a sliver of nail like a creased eye. *Dirty pilgrim.* Polly jerked back, her nipple dislodging from the baby's lips. The red mouth howled with hunger. Revulsion settled over her body, murky and thick, a vernix-coat of shame. The baby strained, turned redder. Polly shivered. She returned the baby to her breast.

A quiet descended upon the bedroom. Some old feeling welled up in Polly as she watched the baby suckling; a distant déjà vu, an odd memory she couldn't quite claim. She glanced once more at her own left thumb—it remained immaculate, human. Polly looked back at the baby sleeping at her breast. She closed her eyes. *You are beautiful,* she murmured as she rocked them both.

Border Crossings

Miriam's problem with her husband started innocently enough, with coffee. Jerry drank too much of it. It wasn't so much his bitter breath, irritability, or sleepless nights away from their bed that bothered her. Mostly, it was the waste of it all. "Sorry, Earth," she would say whenever she opened the door of their coastal blue Subaru sedan. Stained Styrofoam cups littered the passenger-side floor, spilled out of cup holders, collected in perilous stacks between the seats. The Subaru was nearly new, shiny and gleaming on the exterior, but inside it was a dump.

"Are you actively trying to destroy the planet?" she'd asked him more than once. But she never mentioned the expense—presumably considerable at his rate—though, of course, that weighed on her too. Despite a very egalitarian marriage, Jerry was technically the breadwinner. Miriam thought she might bring up the issue of expense later, once she got on track with her personal wellness business, started to actually see a profit from the investment she'd supposedly been making in herself. She was selling shampoo these days, part-time. Of course, it was more than just shampoo. "It's a lifestyle," Tonya, her Market Mentor (and former meditation coach), reminded her. "You're selling yourself."

When Jerry promised to carry a reusable mug, Miriam resolved to drop the issue. But Miriam had a hard time sticking to her convictions; her willpower was a choking, hollow thing. She couldn't stop her own drinking, for example—couldn't resist a glass of wine to relax, a glass to pair with dinner, another to fall asleep. Even though her husband was a rehab counselor. Even though she suspected she might have a problem.

Jerry's newfound beverage habit evened the score, somewhat. But she found the suddenness of his transformation unsettling. One Saturday night, Miriam sat alone at the kitchen counter, swirling the residue from another glass of wine. (Jerry never drank with her, hardly ever touched the stuff, on account of his profession.) It was already eight, and Jerry was reaching for his coat. "You're obsessed," she said over her shoulder. "I thought you hated coffee."

"Blame it on the baby," he said with a receding smile. Their daughter Roxy, fifteen months old, had never been much of a sleeper.

Miriam swiveled in her chair to face him. "Can't you make coffee at home like a normal person?"

"No, and you know why, Miriam," Jerry said, staring at his reflection in the entryway mirror. He removed the delicate black comb that he had taken to keeping in his front shirt pocket, parting his hair in the opposite direction. "I don't like the taste. I can only stomach the girly stuff."

"I thought you were cutting back on sugar."

He didn't respond, just shot her a stony look through the mirror. *This is above your pay grade.* There was something unsettling about the way his eyes blinked back at her, vaguely rodential, as he gathered his keys and left.

*

Three weeks later, Jerry and Miriam sit side by side in their Subaru, stuck behind a hulking pickup on Route 9. Today is their seven-year anniversary, and they are driving to Canada with Roxy. The pickup hauls a jumble of filthy poultry cages, empty and untethered, their metal doors rattling. Black tendrils of smoke rise up through the truck's exhaust. Miriam stares at its dusty mudflaps:

twin silhouettes of naked women reclining, resigned to the mess.

Jerry is curled around the steering wheel, his head pivoting back and forth as he contemplates passing. He edges closer and closer to the truck's rear bumper, when an errant rock dislodges from behind its left mudflap. The rock hits their windshield like spit to the face. "Motherfucker," Jerry sputters. To Miriam, it looks like practically nothing, just a faint indent in the glass, but she knows that by tomorrow it will have spread across the windshield. Somebody will have to repair it. "Fucking new cars never stay that way for long," Jerry says, mostly to himself. Miriam fingers her rose quartz necklace. Stone of calm. Stone of self-love. They keep driving north, Jerry's gaze dead set on the truck, and Miriam looking first to him and then to the road, eyes darting like a wild animal.

*

In meditation class, they call it "monkey mind"—the brain's tendency to bounce from one thought to the next, restless and malcontent. In this way, Miriam replays the exact moment her marriage imploded. Last night, while packing for their anniversary trip, Miriam was rifling through her sock drawer when she received the Facebook message from Chloe. Miriam's suitcase lay open on the bed, half packed and already too full. She set down her glass of wine and reached for her phone. The bedside clock flashed 10:00 PM.

Jerry had recently returned home and now sat watching CNN's coverage of the Hope crisis. A lone American terrorist had detonated a pipe bomb, killing three people at a mining operation in Hope, British Columbia. *The latest in a series of escalating acts of terrorism against Canadian mining companies whose toxic byproducts flow into US tributaries.* Jerry rested his feet on the open flap of Miriam's suitcase, his broad back against the velvet headboard, muttering something about "goddamn eco-fascists." Miriam could smell the coffee coming off him in waves. She'd stopped mentioning it, for good this time. With the bombing, everyone in their small Washington border town had been on edge lately. The talking heads on TV spoke of punitive sanctions, retaliatory actions, escalating violence.

Chloe's message read: *Hi Miriam. You don't know me, but I'm a friend of your husband. He says you and I would be great friends too! That's why I wanted to talk before things got out of hand. Jerry's a sweet guy, and I know he loves you a lot, but...*

As Miriam absorbed the message, the TV commentary receded. She studied a stain on the bedspread, a dark-red starburst, and wondered absently whether it was blood or wine.

*

Miriam pokes at a crimson bruise that blooms across her wrist. In the rearview mirror, Miriam notices Roxy's eyes shut slowly, as a sign over the freeway flashes in harsh orange:

SUMAS-HUNTINGDON BORDER CROSSING – 5 MILES (8 KM) – NO WAIT.

As they approach Canadian customs, there's only one car ahead of them. Miriam holds their passports in her lap, along with Roxy's birth certificate. She swallows, mindlessly tugging at the chain of her necklace. Border crossings make her nervous. Jerry's no help. He wilts under the pressure of interrogation, pausing for uncomfortable lengths, forgetting what he does for a living, his home address. Or he gets giddy, smirking cartoonishly like someone's told a tasteless joke.

They pull up alongside the small roadside booth. Inside sits a customs officer, neatly boxed in, her bronze hair drawn back in an austere ponytail. "Passports," she says briskly, reaching out the window. Miriam passes them to Jerry, dismayed to see his hands twitch as he hands over their documents. If the officer notices, she doesn't say.

"Mr. Taffet? Where are you heading today?"

"Up to Canada...well, Blind Bay, Canada."

"How long will you be staying?"

"Just three nights..."

"Is the trip for business or pleasure?" She has barely looked up from the passports, her pen making discreet scratches on the paper in front of her.

"Pleasure." Jerry is smiling his cheesy smile. Sweat gleams on his temples.

"And what do you do for work, Mr. Taffet?"

"Teen substance abuse."

"I'm sorry?" She looks up from her paperwork, frowning.

"Sorry. I work as a substance abuse counselor with at-risk teenagers." Jerry clears his throat. "At a rehab clinic. All my kids have substance addiction issues...coke, booze, pills, pot, glue, bear tranquilizers...you name it, I help them..."

He's rambling now. Miriam pictures Jerry cradling the drooping head of a bear in his lap, lifting up her soft lip to reveal clenched and burnished teeth. He drags the bear's limp and crumpled body down their driveway, lovingly stuffs it into the trunk of the Subaru. Miriam breathes in deeply, trying to dispel the intrusive image. *Get it together. What is wrong with you?*

"Who else is with you?" The officer lowers her head to look into the open driver's side window.

"I'm Miriam Taffet. We're here with our daughter, Roxanne."

"What do you do for work, Ms. Taffet?" She squints at Miriam.

"I'm a mom," Miriam replies. It feels too short. Lopped off.

The officer smiles for the first time, a tired, conciliatory smile.

"Hardest job there is." Miriam forces a smile back, gaping and insincere. She can't help feeling like something has occurred at her expense.

What do you do? God, Miriam hates that question. *What do you do?* It feels like a set-up. Later tonight, she'll ransack her brain for something else she could have said. Sometimes she flirts with different answers, trying them on like discount-store sunglasses. "I'm a business owner" sounds too pretentious, and "I sell shampoo" makes her feel silly and small. Whatever she comes up with seems, somehow, fraudulent. *What is wrong with you?* she asks again. *When are you going to do something with your life?*

Back in college, Miriam had been an activist, of sorts. She had marched for climate change, protested factory farming. She had been a vegetarian, for a while. At one point, she fancied herself the kind of punk who would rescue caged lab rats, free poor mice covered in mascara or soaked in shampoo. Now she peddles the stuff. College Miriam would have considered her a sell-out—an unsuccessful sell-out at that. Of course, there were a lot of things College Miriam didn't understand: that there is a clock ticking, counting down to the end of everything, and there's nothing you can do to stop it.

"Do you have anything to declare?" the officer asks.

"Uh, I don't think so," says Jerry, drumming his fingers against the steering wheel.

Miriam winces. She wishes he would be slicker, more artful.

"Nothing at all?" the officer asks. Her face is stern and unrelenting.

"No, ma'am?" With his unsteady inflection, it comes off as a question. The officer sets the passports down on the table.

"Pop your trunk, sir." She stands up and exits the booth, disappears behind their car.

Jerry does as he's told. He turns to Miriam and shrugs. In the dozen times they've crossed the border, no one's asked to search their trunk before. *Must be the terrorist attack,* Miriam thinks. Then the officer is back, bending down close to Jerry's open window and pointing ahead.

"Sir, I need you to drive up to that pull-out and park. The officer there will give you further instructions."

"What's happening? I don't think—"

"Sir, drive forward and park your car."

Jerry fumbles with the shift, momentarily sending the car backwards a few feet. As he corrects course, the car lurches forward so fast that they almost pass the pull-out. They park, and there's another officer standing by the curb waiting, watching them.

"Everyone out," he says, rocking back and forth on the heels of his boots. He is younger than the other officer by a decade or more and wears tinted sunglasses even though it's overcast. His pistol hangs close on his hip. "Head inside to the office. Leave your car doors unlocked and the trunk open."

Miriam grabs her purse, scanning the floor for their passports before remembering that the booth officer never returned them. She opens the back door and unbuckles Roxy, red-faced and clammy from her truncated nap. As Miriam grabs the diaper bag, she sees an empty coffee cup on the floor behind the driver's seat. Miriam wonders how long it's been sitting there. With her free hand she inspects it, notices bite marks along its Styrofoam rim.

*

Feet still resting on Miriam's half-packed suitcase, Jerry had come clean while sitting on their ivory bedspread in boxers and socks. "There's something wrong with me," he said, tears streaming. "I don't know why I do the things I do." His body slumped down into the folds of the comforter, heavy like a stone in a lake.

At the beginning, he told Miriam, he had only wanted to help the girl. He was trying to be supportive. Chloe, a charge of his at the rehab clinic, turned eighteen three months ago. Jerry had taken a shine to her immediately: a former foster kid and self-avowed junkie, she was free-spirited and optimistic even though the world had only given her shit in return. She'd had a hell of a time bouncing through the foster care system, Jerry explained with a dim look in his eyes. Her resilience was contagious, admirable really. And of course she was pretty, perhaps strikingly so, if in a strange and self-conscious sort of way, her head too small for the rest of her body, her arms far too skinny, too scarred.

Jerry had been helping Chloe get her life back together, secure a job, keep sober. It wasn't his idea for her to become a bikini barista at XXXpresso—"Where our girls are as hot as our coffee!"—but when she told him about it, eyes sparkling, dopey grin lighting up her narrow face, he couldn't dampen her spirit, could he? This girl who, after everything, was trying her best to get her life back together.

Somewhere along the line, things went off script. He became too invested. He visited her at work, and their conversations moved from her recovery to topics of a more personal nature: her stepfather, ex-boyfriends, casual hookups. At some point, he started tipping her for "XXXtras"—a customer loyalty gimmick—pictures mostly, and a few videos, sent to his phone. He promised Miriam it hadn't gone further than that.

As Jerry related all this, he seemed earnest, contrite. He was sorry for everything, most of all the lies. He answered her questions: yes, he understood he had been chipping away at her trust, in tidy little increments. Yes, he realized he would lose his job if anyone found out. But no, he hadn't been thinking about his job—or Miriam—at the time. Yes, he supposed he might have a "thing" for teenagers. Or he might have some sort of sex addiction, he wasn't sure. One thing Miriam never asked was how much money he'd spent, what it had been worth.

Miriam pored over Chloe's Facebook profile with grim fascination. Opening a second bottle of merlot, Miriam scrolled through countless photos of the girl in various neon tank tops, shorts with four-letter words printed on the ass. In some, Chloe wore her dark hair in limp pigtails that fell past her knobby shoulders. In others, she held her middle finger up towards the camera, aimed at some invisible presence. She didn't smile, just tilted her slight, angled chin up accusatorially.

Jerry covered his eyes like he couldn't bear the pictures, couldn't face Chloe's indicting stare. "Can you ever forgive me?" he asked eventually, eyes swollen and red.

"I tried so hard to be perfect for you," he said through tears.

And eventually: "I never realized how trapped I was."

Miriam said nothing, only finished her wine and crawled under the covers, fully clothed. No one bothered to turn off the television: the latest news on the tightening of the US-Canadian border, the building of walls, the quick deterioration of centuries-long economic partnerships.

"Mir, what are we going to do?" Jerry said, his voice a wail, almost drowned out by the steady hum of the television, but not quite.

*

The inside of the Canadian customs office is claustrophobic, oppressively gray, its surfaces coated with dullness. Straight ahead, three officials sit behind plexiglass barriers, facing computer screens. The only other civilian in sight stands up front, holding a cardboard box and talking in hushed tones with another official. No one looks up when the American family enters, even as Roxy's unflagging shrieks echo against the windowless walls. Miriam and Jerry take a seat on the monochrome plastic chairs by the entrance, unsure of what to do next. Miriam holds Roxy on her lap, both arms wrapped tightly around her relentless, writhing body. To her right, Miriam can see a long hall lined with doors. All shut. Muffled voices emerge periodically, vague and ghostly.

She bounces Roxy on her leg as she repeats to herself: *I can do hard things. I can do hard things.* This is her self-empowerment mantra. She first saw it on the Instagram feed of a yoga instructor she used to follow, until an onslaught of photos from her tropical vacation made Miriam feel uncharitable. The mantra is meant to instill calm in difficult times, but Miriam has yet to reap its intended effect.

"Should we tell someone we're here?" Jerry asks her a little too loudly. His leg is bobbing up and down, another coffee-addled habit.

"I'm sure they can see us," she whispers. "Just wait."

"No harm in asking." But he doesn't get up. Instead, he sighs intermittently, occasionally shaking his head or leaning forward exaggeratedly to check the wall clock to their left.

Miriam wonders where all the people are. The building seems strangely deserted. Even though it's one of the smaller crossings, there should be more activity. It's practically rush hour.

"Jerry Taffet." Startled, Miriam and Jerry stand up in unison and head to an open counter where a bulky, blond officer beckons. He has an imposing scar jutting from lip to nose, making him look snarling and dissatisfied. His badge reads, "Tremblay." Miriam has the fleeting urge to pray, something she hasn't done since she was fourteen.

Jerry and Miriam stand close together, not touching. Miriam grips the edge of the counter to steady herself. She doesn't do well in these sorts of high-stress situations with unknown variables.

"Sir, we've found evidence indicating an intent to cross the border into Canada for illegal purposes."

Jerry coughs—a wet, out-of-control sputter. It seems to take an incredibly long time for him to regain composure. What had he done, and how had Miriam failed to see it? She thinks of the pictures that must still be on his phone. The bite marks on the coffee cups. Damning evidence of a crime she can't fully name.

"Illegal purposes?" Miriam repeats, turning to Jerry. "What's he talking about?"

"I have no earthly idea. I just don't..." His shoulders sag. He looks at her wide-eyed, his voice barely a whisper.

Miriam turns back to Tremblay and says, "Like we told the first officer, we're here on vacation. It's our anniversary." Roxy squirms and tries to grab for a pen on the counter.

The officer grimaces, recording some accusation with his keyboard. *You have nothing to be scared of. Nothing,* she repeats to herself. Jerry stands there shaking his head in slow motion.

Tremblay keeps typing. "Have we done something wrong?" Miriam asks, to no one in particular. She tries to keep her voice even.

The officer looks up from his computer, with a hazy, bored blink. "Ma'am, our officers found eight boxes of consumer products in the trunk of your vehicle."

Jerry turns to her with a slight, almost imperceptible smile. The fucking shampoo. Miriam covers her mouth with her hand, puts it back down on the counter.

"It's unlawful to bring undeclared products into Canada for sale," the officer continues. His scar has a shiny, iridescent quality, like mirror glass.

"I must have forgotten to take out my inventory before we

drove up. We were in a rush," Miriam says. "I sell hemp-based beauty products. Part-time—for Good Karma Wellness." Tremblay leans back in his chair, crossing his arms. As the officer holds her gaze, she can sense Jerry aggressively rubbing his temples in her peripheral vision. "It was an honest mistake. We weren't going to sell anything."

Tremblay looks at her as if looking through a window pane. *It's just eight boxes*, she thinks, *how much trouble can it be?* The look in the officer's eyes reveals nothing.

"Okay. Have a seat," he says.

"How long will this take?" Jerry says, abruptly. Miriam kicks at his shoe as hard as she can without making a sound.

Tremblay shakes his head. "This is a serious offense, sir. You're going to be here awhile." Jerry clears his throat. "Take a seat," Tremblay insists. "This will go much better if you cooperate." Miriam nods vigorously and then pulls Jerry away by the back of his shirt.

They return to their plastic chairs. Behind them, the clock ticks and ticks with incessant, indifferent strokes.

Miriam contemplates the end of her marriage. She's never been opposed to divorce, philosophically speaking, and has always carried an acute awareness of the prospect in her mind. She knows the percentages, and she's not stupid enough to think that she and Jerry are an exceptional couple. But now the thought chills her, fills her with dread, like the slow slide of a conveyor belt down into darkness, single file. She thinks of all those shampoo bottles, some stacked neatly in the back of their garage, others still in boxes in the Subaru's trunk. Idly waiting for her. All eventually destined for the landfill. This thing that was supposed to set her free now feels like rocks lodged deep in her coat pockets.

*

Last night, after Jerry's confession, Miriam couldn't stop thinking about the damn shampoo. As Jerry stroked her back with unrelenting apologies, she thought of the new inventory order she'd placed the day before, only her second since joining on as a Market Partner. One hundred high-end bottles costing over $4,000. Eco-friendly and cruelty free. She hadn't made a dent in the first shipment, her "personal investment starter kit," but Tonya advised her to double down, assured her "just when you feel like you're about to go under is when you start growing your business in earnest." She spoke from personal experience, Tonya confided.

Miriam felt a fresh wave of shame thinking about how she succumbed to the pressure of Tonya's "hustle harder" insistence. The dangled promises of "sisterhood" and "freedom from the corporate rat race." Worse, Jerry didn't bat an eye when she told him, after the fact, that the upfront payment had been more than she'd expected. Much more. He trusted her, knew she would make him proud. My little entrepreneur, he called her. Of course, she never mentioned to him that maybe this had been a mistake. That she had the sensation of being buried alive under the weight of all those "life-changing" bottles.

Miriam pulled the ivory bedspread over her shoulders. Jerry leaned in to kiss her, and this time she let him. It felt like kissing someone else, had a forbidden, alien quality to it. Miriam entertained that feeling for a few brief moments, until it was overtaken by an image in her mind, played as if on a screen: Jerry sitting sweat-faced in the Subaru, window rolled down and car idling. Chloe, captive inside the drive-thru booth, sports a peach bikini and a gleaming belly button ring. The espresso machine spits creamy white foam into another Styrofoam cup, as Jerry takes out a twenty from his wallet, fingers twitching. Chole bends out the booth window, contorting the top half of her body across the frame so he can delicately place the bill where the bikini elastic meets the sunlit skin of her breast. She brushes back the freshly dyed hair that's fallen over her face and swivels her torso around, efficient as an assembly line. Jerry sits and watches, rapt and marveling and thinking nothing of Miriam. His wedding ring makes a hollow thunk as it meets back with the steering wheel.

Miriam shook the image from her mind, burying her head in the pillow as Jerry continued to stroke her back. He spoke about renewing their vows, how beautiful she looked, and how much he still wanted her. Miriam felt weighed down by the wine, as Jerry's promises ebbed in and out of her consciousness.

Then he was on top of her, pinning her hands against the bed, like she'd been asking him to do for years, but he had always demurred, saying it felt "wrong." She moved to push him off her back, bracing both hands against the bed for leverage but, uncharacteristically, he didn't budge. He was solid, hard and unyielding. When he entered her, she was actually wet for once. She could feel him inside her, but the sensation was muted and hazy, like her entire body was covered in gauze. The black hole receded into the distance, if only for a moment.

He took one broad hand against the back of her head and pressed her face into the pillow, his fingers hooking into her hair, his knuckles hard against her scalp. "Filthy little crack whore," he spat, and she came.

After, Jerry laid his head on Miriam's chest. She parted his damp hair with her fingers, whispering her own promises and trying not to think about whether she would keep them.

Dawn crept in through the blinds. Miriam decided they would go to Canada as planned, rather than waste their deposit on the cabin. Jerry crammed their hastily packed suitcases into the backseat of the car, and they drove north.

Miriam stares at the wall calendar that hangs behind the customs counter. *Save the Great White North*: a Mountie with a stoic, chiseled jaw and scarlet uniform, framed by towering evergreens topped with snow. Something in the Mountie's unwavering gaze reminds her of church.

"I SWEAR TO GOD!" A voice reverberates through the dark hallway, from behind some closed door. It cuts through the clicking of pens and shuffling of paperwork; a man wailing, a low and guttural cry. Miriam and Jerry look to each other. The wailing crescendos, followed by the sound of chairs scraping frantically across hard floors, something angular crashing against a wall. The door closest to them snaps open. A lanky, boyish officer emerges from the frame, pistol ready at his side. The officers at the counter immediately get to their feet and rush over. Another officer lurches past, fumbling with the snap that secures his gun in its holster.

With the door still open, Miriam can hear the first voice: "I swear to God! I haven't done anything wrong. I haven't done anything!"

"Sir, you cannot carry a concealed weapon across the border!"

"I didn't know, I swear!" The voice slurs back into a wail.

"I found a double-bladed knife in his coat pocket when I searched him," the boyish officer says.

"Sir, do you have any other weapons on you? Any explosives?"

Two officers emerge from the door, holding the shouting man's arms behind him. The man is disheveled, nothing but bones and wild eyes, wearing a weathered shirt that urges, "Save Our Streams." He blinks frantically, insisting, "I haven't done anything—you're hurting me—I haven't done anything," as officers lead him farther down the hall. His cries fade, and there's only the sound of soles passing through hidden corridors. *This is hell*, Miriam thinks. *I'm in hell and I'm never going to get out.* She wills herself to be rational, but the thought stuns her like a bolt through the brain.

"We shouldn't be here," Jerry says. "I should go back and talk to them, ask them to move us somewhere else. This isn't safe."

"Are you kidding?" Miriam shoots back. "That'll only make things worse."

"This is unacceptable," Jerry continues. "Unsafe and unacceptable. That man, Miriam! That man had a weapon and he was standing right next to us!"

"Don't," she says through clenched teeth. "Just don't."

Roxy has started crying again. Miriam begins rocking her in the crook of her arm like a newborn. Roxy struggles against the unnatural hold.

"They had their guns drawn—we could have been shot! And we've been sitting here for hours. Christ, somebody has to do something," Jerry flashes a disapproving look at Miriam, then Roxy, but he doesn't move.

Roxy is howling now as Miriam rocks her faster. "You aren't capable of doing anything," Miriam says, keeping her voice low. "That's how we got here, right? An officer asks you if you have anything to declare, and you say, 'Uh, I don't *think* so?' You see a woman in a booth and you just can't keep it together."

"How is this my fault? It's your shampoo. For your so-called business." He spits out the word *business* like it's rotten.

"Maybe if you weren't so preoccupied with fucking teenagers, I could have actually focused on my business."

He turns red and says nothing, only blinks at her. Finally, he mutters under his breath, "It's just shampoo, Miriam."

*

Miriam's phone buzzes from deep in her coat pocket, and she rushes for it, desperate for a distraction. *Another mindless impulse,* she chastises herself. Miriam knows she is always grasping for something, filling her life with *things*. Mantras, poses, products—all designed to distract from the fact she is just sitting here waiting for something to happen. Accumulating broken promises, boxing herself into smaller and smaller spaces, all the while watching her available options winnow down to nothing. It's as if she's been staring so long through the bars of her cage that pretty soon they're all she can see.

It's another message from Chloe: *Hey! Hope this isn't out of line, but I saw you sell Good Karma? I'd love to try something new, I hate my hair! Lemme know! xoxox Chloe.*

What could Miriam possibly say? She feels a ridiculous urge to gather up Chloe, with her belly button ring and her scars, and apologize to her. Smooth out her pigtails and tell her not to worry, explain that this has all been one awful misunderstanding. Some sisterhood, this. Still, Miriam senses she has some advice to give, some encouragement, if only she could uncover it herself.

Miriam stops. After a moment, she will return her phone to her pocket, loosen her hold on Roxy. Above Jerry, she'll notice a window, one she'd have sworn wasn't there before. Miriam will wonder what else she's missed, sitting here. As she peers down the dark hallway and back towards her future, ticking away like a bomb.

Acknowledgments

Many thanks to the editors and staff of the following journals for first publishing several of the stories that appear in this collection:

Apalachee Review, "The New Jenny"

Briar Cliff Review, "It's No Fun Anymore"

CALYX Journal, "Border Crossings"

Typehouse Magazine, "Estate Sale"

Variant Literature, "Thumb Stump"

Witness Magazine, "From the Waist Down"

This book is dedicated to my husband—my partner and first reader. Your love and time and support mean the world to me. Thank you for seeing this through.

My love and thanks to Lenore Micka-Foos, who has inspired me to write since the day she was born. You are magic. And to Kayla and Jesse Ericksen, for understanding and encouraging me in ways that only siblings can. Special thanks to my mom, Jodi, who taught me how to read and what books are for.

Thanks to all those who read my work and offered their unwavering support and reassurances along the way, in coffee-houses and workshops and Zoom meetings. To my writing friends: Seema Balwani, Olivia Haberman, Christina Holt, Alice Kinerk, Nicole McGrath, and Ethel Sweed. Lauren Allen for sticking with me through many early drafts and ever-evolving writing groups. Ellen Foos for providing proofreading, good advice, and precious time to write over the years. Thanks to Hugo House, The Rice Place, and The Writers' Colony at Dairy Hollow for providing me with guidance, space, and support to finish this manuscript. To my writing teachers: Scott Driscoll, Becky Mandelbaum, and Peter Mountford—along with so much else, you showed me how it's done. And to The Writer's Center, Chuckanut Writers, and HamLit for their kindness and encouragement early in my writing journey.

And finally, tremendous gratitude to the team at Apprentice House—Kevin Atticks, Molly Clement, Olivia Cresser, Molly Gerard, and Natalie Misyak. Thank you for making my dream come true. I'm forever grateful for this opportunity.

About the Author

Brittany Micka-Foos is a writer living in the Pacific Northwest. She is the author of the poetry chapbook *a litany of words as fragile as window glass* (Bottlecap Press, 2024). Her work has been published in *Ninth Letter*, *Witness Magazine*, *NonBinary Review*, *CALYX*, and elsewhere.

To read more, visit: www.brittanymickafoos.com.

Apprentice
House Press
Loyola University Maryland

Apprentice House is the country's only campus-based, student-staffed book publishing company. Directed by professors and industry professionals, it is a nonprofit activity of the Communication Department at Loyola University Maryland.

Using state-of-the-art technology and an experiential learning model of education, Apprentice House publishes books in untraditional ways. This dual responsibility as publishers and educators creates an unprecedented collaborative environment among faculty and students, while teaching tomorrow's editors, designers, and marketers.

Eclectic and provocative, Apprentice House titles intend to entertain as well as spark dialogue on a variety of topics. Financial contributions to sustain the press's work are welcomed. Contributions are tax deductible to the fullest extent allowed by the IRS.

To learn more about Apprentice House books or to obtain submission guidelines, please visit www.apprenticehouse.com.

Apprentice House Press
Communication Department
Loyola University Maryland
4501 N. Charles Street
Baltimore, MD 21210
Ph: 410-617-5265
info@apprenticehouse.com • www.apprenticehouse.com

www.ingramcontent.com/pod-product-compliance
Lightning Source LLC
Chambersburg PA
CBHW071440260626
47170CB00008B/2782